PERLOO

THE BOLD

PERLOO

THE BOLD

AVI

SCHOLASTIC PRESS • NEW YORK

Copyright ©1998 by Avi. All rights reserved. Published by Scholastic Press, a division of Scholastic Inc., *Publishers since 1920*. SCHOLASTIC PRESS and associated logos are trademarks and/or registered trademarks of Scholastic Inc.

LIBRARY OF CONGRESS CATALOGING-IN-PUBLICATION DATA

Avi, 1937–
Perloo the bold / by Avi—1st ed.
p.   cm.
Summary: Perloo, a peaceful scholar who has been chosen to succeed Jolaine as leader of the furry underground people called the Montmers, finds himself in danger when Jolaine dies and her evil son seizes control of the burrow.

ISBN 0-590-11002-0

[1. Fantasy.]   II. Title.
PZ7.A953Las   1998   [Fic]–DC21   97-10681

10 9 8 7 6 5 4 3 2 1   8 9/9 0/0 01 02

Printed in the U.S.A.   23
First edition, November 1998
The text type was set in Bembo 13.5/17.
Book design by Marijka Kostiw

FOR ROBERT

TABLE OF

CONTENTS

PERLOO

THE BOLD

PERLOO

THICKLY FALLING SNOW, tossed and turned by wailing winds, filled the air with streaky blurs of white and gray. It was hard to see. It was hard to move. It was even hard to breathe.

Despite the weather, a young female Montmer by the name of Lucabara came hurtling down the eastern slope of Rasquich Mountain as fast as she could ski on her long, flat feet. In one paw she carried a tall, sharply pointed pole known as a pike.

As Lucabara sped down the mountainside she paused now and again to look anxiously back, making sure she was not being followed. Only then did she continue on.

At the bottom of Glentick Dell she reached her destination: a mound of earth so deeply buried in snow it looked like the top half of a snowball.

In haste she searched for a smoke pipe, but when she found it there was no sign of either smoke or heat. Increasingly anxious, she used her four-fingered paws to hurriedly wipe away the snow until she uncovered a small wooden door at the top of the mound. On the door a name had been crudely written:

Perloo

After checking once more to make certain she was not being observed, Lucabara banged on the door. "Perloo!" she called. "If you're there, let me in! It's *important*."

The call echoed down a long, dark, earthen tunnel until it reached the larger room of a two-room burrow. There, fast asleep on a bed of dry moss, dreaming of the daring deeds of ancient Montmers, lay Perloo.

Perloo was three hops high and twelve years new —just about the same as Lucabara. But while her ears were slender and pointed at the tips, his were wide and bulging. He had a broad face, a mouth with a poky lower lip, and a nose of delicate pink. Lucabara's nose was blue.

As a female Montmer, Lucabara had a hair tuft at the nape of her neck. Perloo—a male—had whiskers, much like a rabbit's but thicker, and quite scruffy. As for Perloo's unshod feet, they were just like Lucabara's: long as he was tall, very narrow, very flat.

Like all Montmers, Perloo's plump body was covered—neck to ankle—with short, rough, curly fur. In the thin, cold mountain air the fur was not enough to keep warm. That was why Montmers wore loose-fitting smocks made of animal skins—fur side out.

Perloo's smock had been made from beaver skin. While sleeping he had tucked head, body, knobby knees, long feet, two stubby arms, and paws inside it. The only part of him exposed to the air was one of his jackrabbit-like ears. It stuck straight up and out of his smock so as to catch any unusual sound. Which is how he heard Lucabara's call.

"Oh, bird's teeth," Perloo muttered to himself as he rubbed his baggy eyes and scratched his unkempt whiskers. "Who could possibly want *me?*"

Reluctantly, he pawed the neck string of his smock open. It allowed his head to pop out, thus freeing his nose to sniff. Though he tried to smell who might be calling, the scent proved too weak.

Mumbling "bother" under his breath, Perloo groped in the dark until he found some flints beneath a pile of bark books. He struck a spark and lit a candle, which brought pale yellow light to the snug burrow room.

"Perloo, are you there?" the call continued. "If you are, you must let me in!"

Never a fast mover, Perloo loosened the bottom string of his smock, lowered his flat feet down to the dirt floor, and stood upon his skinny legs. His ear tips brushed the ceiling where roots—like wandering fingers—dangled through the earth.

Breathing sleepily of the musty air, Perloo grasped the burning candle and hopped up the tunnel to the burrow door, where a peephole allowed him to see who was outside. There were all kinds of animals on the

mountain—goats, rabbits, coyotes, among others—
but it was the bears, wolves, and mountain lions that
concerned Montmers. Of even greater danger were
the Felbarts, the Montmers' particular enemies.

Though as far as Perloo knew there was peace between the tribes, Montmers considered Felbarts to be
dangerous, always capable of deceit. Which was why
Perloo took the time to flip open the peephole and
look outside. Only when he saw the twin tips of
Montmer ears did he release the safety peg and let the
door drop down. There was Lucabara, smock covered
with snow, icicles hanging from her ears.

"What took you so long?" she asked, giving Perloo
a reproachful glare. "Were you reading?"

Perloo blinked. "Do I know you?" he asked.

"I'm Lucabara," she replied brusquely. "I live in the
Central Tribe Burrow. Though we haven't met, I've
heard a great deal about you."

"You do? You have?" Perloo said, rubbing his paws
nervously while wondering why this unfamiliar female was visiting.

Lucabara gave a vigorous shake to rid herself of
snow and ice, then hopped right down the doorway,
set her pike against the wall, plucked the candle from
Perloo's paws, and bounded down his tunnel.

A flustered Perloo pushed the door up against the
wind and snow, then hastened to follow. When he
caught up to his visitor she was standing in the middle of his main room, holding his candle high, looking
about with intense interest.

Perloo's furnishings were quite ordinary: moss bed, low table, foot mat of woven grass. On one wall hung a picture of Mogwat the Magpie, Great Teaching Bird of the Montmers. Mogwat had a blue-black back; white breast; bright, beady eyes; a long tail; and a sharp black beak. Her head was cocked to one side, as if ever ready to see, hear, and tell all. Montmers loved to quote her sayings.

Except for the bed—where Perloo did most of his reading—the burrow was crowded with bark books. Against the earthen walls were shelves packed helter-skelter. All the books were about Montmer history or mythology.

Opposite the bed, a small, stone-faced fireplace had been built into the earth. A lumpy clay pot, half full of water, hung from a stone hook, but the hearth—also stuffed with books—was cold.

"What a mess," Lucabara proclaimed as she loosened the neck string of her smock.

"It's just me," Perloo murmured apologetically. He was not accustomed to company. "Can . . . can I get you some myrtle tea?"

"I don't think we have time," Lucabara replied.

Perloo, wondering what Lucabara could possible mean, muttered, "There's always time for tea and honey."

"If you hurry," she agreed, pushing some books off the mat and squatting down. Then she just stared at Perloo.

Uncomfortable beneath her gaze, Perloo hurried

into his storeroom. Being mid–Coldcross it was only half full of nuts, roots, and dried vegetables. As for his stock of honey, he suddenly remembered he'd used it up and never had replaced it.

Nonetheless he hopped back to the fireplace with myrtle sprig and cups in paw. Rather clumsily he removed the books and struggled to light a fire. "How deep is the snow?" he asked, trying to make polite conversation.

"Maybe seven hops since sun-up," Lucabara replied. "And still coming down."

"The worst snow was the Great Blizzard in the Frog Year," Perloo informed her. "Twelve hops in one sun-glow," he said, using the Montmer term for a twenty-four-hour period. When Lucabara said nothing, Perloo, fearful that she thought he had been showing off his knowledge, hastened to add, "At least that's what I read . . . somewhere."

The fire ablaze, Perloo set the water to boil. Soon the sweet scent of myrtle began to perfume the room.

Lucabara lifted one of her long, bare feet and rubbed it. "Perloo," she said, "why didn't you have a fire going?"

"I was sleeping," he said.

"I thought all you did was read," she said.

"I *was* reading," Perloo admitted. "A fine book too, *The Way of Montmer Heroes*. But . . . I fell asleep."

Lucabara looked at him keenly. "Perloo," she said, "Mogwat taught us that 'A life without challenge is a life not lived.' What about you? Do you like challenges?"

"I don't think so," Perloo admitted. The very thought of challenges made him nervous. "Why do you ask?"

"Perloo," Lucabara said, "Granter Jolaine is very ill."

"Oh, my!" Perloo exclaimed. "Is . . . is that why you came? To tell me that?"

"Yes."

"I'm awfully sorry to hear it," Perloo declared, so troubled he absentmindedly took a sip of the tea he had made for his guest. "Did you know," he said, "though it's been a while, I've enjoyed talking to Jolaine. She may be our leader, but she knows more Montmer history than anyone else. More than all my books combined."

Lucabara nodded solemnly but gave no response.

Perloo started to take another sip of tea, only to remember he had made it for Lucabara. He began to offer it to her, then realized it was too late—he had drunk from it. He put it down nervously and said, "How ill is she?"

Lucabara said, "It's probably fatal."

"Oh, dry dust," Perloo whispered. "*Very* dry dust." He stared down at his bare feet. "It's not for nothing that she's been called, 'Jolaine the Good,' " he murmured.

"Perloo," Lucabara said, pausing to take a deep

breath before continuing, "Jolaine has been asking for you."

"*Me?*" Perloo cried.

"When she woke this early," Lucabara explained, "she asked to see you as soon as possible. That's why I came."

"But—but why should she want me?" Perloo stammered in astonishment. His baggy eyes were open very wide now.

"Perloo," Lucabara said firmly, "she told me to say that seeing you was a matter of life and death. And Perloo, she didn't mean *her* life and death. She was speaking of our entire Montmer tribe."

LUCABARA'S NEWS

CHAPTER 2

A BAFFLED PERLOO rubbed his paws. "Can't you tell me more?" he asked.

"All I can say," Lucabara replied carefully, "is that she's very old. Almost fifty. Quite close to death."

"But . . . but why . . . me?" Perloo repeated.

When Lucabara merely gazed at him Perloo half expected her to quote one of Mogwat's sayings, perhaps, "Knowing the length of a Montmer's ear won't tell you if he can listen."

Suddenly he said, "But what about Berwig? Does he want Jolaine to see me?"

Lucabara started. "Why do you even ask?"

"Well, he *is* Jolaine's only cub. And, I presume, the next granter. And if Jolaine is so close to death—" Perloo faltered. "I just don't want to intrude in family matters."

"I've no idea what Berwig thinks," Lucabara replied.

"How come she picked you to get me?" Perloo asked.

"I'm her first assistant."

Perloo's eyes widened again. "You are?"

Lucabara sniffed. "Didn't you know?"

Perloo's pink nose turned purple with embarrassment. "I . . . I don't keep up with things," he admitted. "My reading, and living alone. . . . It's the way I am."

"Then how did you start meeting with Jolaine in the first place?" Lucabara asked.

"It was her idea, not mine. She must have heard about my books. And my reading. She sent for me. We talked about history. It became a regular thing. For a while."

"When did you see her last?"

"Now that you mention it, it's been some time," Perloo said vaguely.

"She's been ill for some time," Lucabara said.

"I didn't know," Perloo said, flustered. "I . . . well, you see it was always *she* who invited me. I would never presume to invite myself. When I didn't hear from her I just thought she didn't want to talk to me anymore."

An awkward silence filled the burrow. Perloo sensed that Lucabara was holding back something. Surely, as Jolaine's first assistant, she would know why the granter wanted him.

"Perloo," she said, as if reading his mind, "if you want to know why Jolaine needs to see you, don't you think you'd best go to her?"

Perloo scratched himself between the ears. The truth was he hated leaving his burrow during Coldcross. It was freezing outside. Inside he had his books to read, roots to nibble, and hot tea, sweet or not. Then he realized what he was thinking. "Forgive me," he murmured, "I'm as heartless as a dead twig. Of course I'll see her."

"Then let's go," Lucabara urged. She stood, flicked her neck tuft high and drew her smock string tight.

Feeling he had little choice, Perloo took a final swallow of the tea, adjusted his smock, took up the candle, and headed for the tunnel.

"What about your fire?" Lucabara asked.

"It'll keep till I get back," Perloo assured her. "I'm sure Jolaine won't keep me long."

Lucabara said nothing.

Perloo, still trying to puzzle out why Jolaine would want him—and she on her deathbed—hopped up the tunnel. Mind only on his mission, he pulled the door open to be rewarded by a burst of snow and wind that extinguished his candle. He had forgotten about the storm.

"Bird's fir," he said to himself and slammed the door shut. Lucabara snorted.

Leaving the gutted candle beneath the door against his return, Perloo drew his smock neck string tighter, then groped in the dark for the door again. This time when he opened it he did so cautiously.

The entire world was white. So thick with snow was both sky and ground it was difficult to know where one ended and the other began. As for the intensity of the cold, it took Perloo's breath away.

"Don't you carry a pike?" he heard Lucabara ask.

Though standing only a few hops from him, she appeared as little more than a smudge.

"I'm not much of a hunter," he explained. "Besides, my pike is broken."

Perloo thought Lucabara gave a little shake of her head. "I'll break the snow," she said.

"Don't get too far in front," he called. "You're hard to see."

"Keep your eyes open," she suggested and started off.

This Lucabara isn't nice at all, Perloo thought. All he said, however, was, "I'll try!"

Since Perloo's burrow was situated in a dell, they had to climb out of it. In good weather, ten easy hops would have sufficed. But now the deep, driving snow made the going difficult.

Having no pike, Perloo had to extend his stubby arms out to either side for balance. Then he spread his long, bare feet into a wide stance and began to hop clumsily uphill.

It was hard going. The cascading snow, whipped by wild winds, came at him from all directions at once. Seeing was difficult. Hearing and smelling were diminished too. Perloo could only hope it would be better when they got out of the dell.

It proved worse. Though the snow no longer swirled, it came at him in an unceasing barrage of what felt like tiny ice pellets. It was either bend over or be blinded. But when he bent down he could see very little. The result was he kept bobbing up and down like a bird pecking seeds.

"Here we go!" he heard Lucabara shout. The next moment she was skiing down the mountainside.

"This better be important," Perloo mumbled as he flexed his skinny legs, leaned slightly forward over his long, flat feet, jutted his head forward so he could see —or at least try to see—thrust his ears back for a streamlined effect, and pushed off. Quickly gathering speed, he skied down the mountainside.

They soon entered an area thickly forested by lodgepole pines. Towering trees—like columns— seemed to be holding up the sky. Though the pressure of the wind was less amidst the trees, Perloo had to struggle to avoid hitting their trunks. Simultaneously, he tried to keep Lucabara in sight. It was not easy. She was a fine skier. He was not. Even so, they continued on, hopping up inclines, skiing down slopes.

Once, trying to avoid a large, twisted aspen tree, Perloo tumbled. The snow, soft and powdery, seemed to swallow him whole. Legs and arms flailing, he struggled to regain the surface. It was hard to dig upward, fall forward, and—all at the same time—haul himself up with his stubby arms. When he finally managed to right himself, Lucabara was standing before him, snorting.

"What's so funny?" Perloo scowled with frustration.

"You look like a centipede going twelve different directions at once."

"I'm just out of practice," Perloo grumbled.

"I'll get you a lesson book," Lucabara returned with a teasing glance.

Irritated by her teasing, Perloo snatched up some snow, packed a snowball, and heaved it at her. His aim was perfect, striking her right between the ears.

At first taken aback, Lucabara grinned, did a jump turn, and sped off.

For a moment Perloo stared after her. What, he asked himself, had gotten into him? Throwing snowballs! That was for cubs.

They skied down three more ridges—Perloo only tumbled once more—then began the long and final climb. It was hard work, but at last Lucabara announced, "Here we are."

Perloo, so bent over with climbing he'd paid little mind to their location, looked up. The Central Tribe Burrow, the biggest burrow in the territory, loomed over their heads.

"We'll use a side entrance," Lucabara said. When they reached it, however, it was closed. Lucabara frowned. "It was open when I left," she said. "I'm afraid we'll have to use the main entrance." They hopped around.

As they drew close a voice from the sentry post at the top of the burrow barked, "Halt! Who approaches?"

Lucabara and Perloo looked up. Two Montmer

sentries—bulky in thick smocks and wood slab chest armor, their pikes armed with thorns—were peering down at them.

"It's me. Lucabara!"

"Who's that with you?"

Perloo was about to shout out his name when Lucabara hastily put a paw in front of his mouth and called, "A friend."

"You may pass."

Lucabara hesitated. "Under whose command are you?" she inquired.

"Berwig's."

Lucabara grunted, but said no more. Hopping silently, she led Perloo to the burrow entryway. As she put paw to door, Perloo, suddenly feeling nervous, said, "Lucabara, what's happening? Why did you try the side entrance? Why didn't you want me to say my name? How come there are sentries posted? I thought I saw their pikes tipped with thorns. Are we at war with the Felbarts again?"

"I don't think so," Lucabara said.

"But you know why Jolaine asked me to come, don't you?"

"Shhh!" Lucabara warned. "You'll speak to her soon." Then, in a grim tone she added—mostly to herself—"I hope."

BERWIG THE BIG

INSIDE THE BURROW Lucabara flung her pike against the wall midst many other pikes, then began to hop hurriedly down a wide, well-lit tunnel. Perloo, brushing off the snow that had encrusted his smock, scrambled to follow.

Though burrowed through the earth, the tunnel had vaulted ceilings. Its walls were smooth and covered with elaborate paintings of Montmer life with a particular emphasis on the wars against the Felbarts. Mogwat was to be seen everywhere, helping the Montmers. The art was illuminated by sputtering beeswax candles stuck in holes in the walls. The flickering light gave the paintings life.

On the floors lay intricately woven grass rugs of many colors. Here and there stood smoldering pots of aromatic herbs and spices, an attempt to reduce the mustiness of the subterranean air.

After some thirty hops, Lucabara and Perloo came upon a door set into the side of the tunnel. Before it stood a Montmer warrior. He was in armor: a slab of wood strapped over his chest and wood stripes bound by leather thongs to protect the tops of his long feet. In one paw he held a long wooden pike. It too was tipped with thorns.

"We need to go this way," Lucabara whispered to Perloo. "It's the fastest way to Jolaine." She reached for the door only to have the warrior bar her way.

"Not permitted," he barked.

"Don't you know who I am?" Lucabara asked.

"Lucabara, Jolaine's first assistant."

"Well?" she said, as if her title was authority enough.

"Sorry," the warrior snapped. "This door remains closed. By order of Berwig."

Perloo looked to Lucabara.

"Follow me," she whispered with ill-concealed anger as she continued down the tunnel. Perloo, glancing back over his shoulder at the warrior, tried to keep up.

"Something *is* wrong," he whispered to Lucabara, "isn't it?"

"The hall will be crowded," was her reply. "It's late feed time."

The Great Hall was the very center of the tribe's life. A vast room, it was used for communal dining, important general meetings, even army musters. Everything was made bright by an array of burning candles as well as large fires blazing in hearths at both sides of the hall. Midst more smoking pots of herbs and spices stood a score of warriors, pikes on the ready. Perloo was puzzled. In his previous visits to

Jolaine there had never been so many warriors.

It was in the Great Hall, at the farthest end, that the tribe throne—the Settop—was placed on a raised platform. Made of stone, the Settop was not just old, it was sacred to Montmers. In all the Montmer territory it was the only sitting apparatus. The granter sat on it when presiding over official and ceremonial gatherings. All other Montmers squatted. Over it hung a carving of Mogwat.

At the moment it was unoccupied.

Mid-hall stood a very long table, laden with wooden trenchers heaped with grasses, roasted roots, nuts, and seeds. Steaming mugs of teas, bowls of thick grain effusions of one kind or another, as well as clay pots of clotted honey were everywhere. The room shimmered with savory warmth.

Squatting before both sides of the table, hunched over food that they were devouring paw to mouth, were some eighty Montmers. Male and female, along with a fair number of cubs, they were clothed in a variety of fur smocks. All were bent forward, long ears crisscrossed across the table like a row of interleaved pikes.

Since talking while eating was considered bad manners among Montmers, none spoke. It was the sound of steady munching and grinding of food that filled the hall. Now and again, one of the eaters sat up straight and, with an intense—if vacant—gaze, jawed furiously at his food.

As Perloo and Lucabara hopped down the length

of the hall, no one paid them any mind. But at the far end of the room, at the head of the table, a large stout Montmer popped up his head. It was Berwig, Jolaine's cub.

Larger than most Montmers—he was known as Berwig the Big—Berwig wore a smock of thick, white fur, which, at the moment, was spotted with bits of food. His cheeks bulged so they obscured his eyes, giving him a constant squint. His whiskers—colored black with acorn dye—were elaborate, consisting of two long, braided strands that extended to either side of his slack mouth before drooping down to his small chin. His ears were fat. On his long paws he wore a multitude of chunky gold bracelets.

First he noticed Lucabara, then Perloo. The moment he saw Perloo his pink nose turned deep purple and his ears began to tremble. In haste, he ducked his head and conferred with the Montmer at his side. After a quick nod Berwig stood up.

All eating ceased. Every Montmer stared at Berwig with brown-eyed intensity.

Nose quivering, glossy ears shaking like aspen leaves, Berwig hopped awkwardly to where Perloo and Lucabara were standing. Just behind him crept the old Montmer with whom he had conferred. Senyous was his name, and he moved like a clinging shadow.

Small, even for a Montmer, Senyous's face was cramped and pinched, as if he had just consumed a dish of pickled sour grass. He was tattered. He limped. He insinuated.

Ever respectful, Perloo hastily pulled down his left ear. "May the sun rise clear over your mountain," he said to Berwig.

Berwig grinned nervously, revealing a mouth of gapped teeth. "Well, well," he said in a loud, abrasive voice. "Here's Lucabara. How nice to see you. Who's your friend?"

"His name is Perloo," she said.

"*Perloo*," Berwig repeated, staring squinty eyed at Perloo, even as his ears continued to shake. "Berwig is *my* name. Berwig the Big!" He broke into a high-pitched, nervous snort, his eyes shifting from Perloo to Lucabara then back again to Perloo.

"Care for something to eat?" he asked. "Just help yourself. Any friend of Lucabara is a friend of mine. I'm in charge, so naturally, anything I say goes."

"Oh, thank you, no," Perloo returned. "I don't want to trouble anyone. I only came because Granter Jolaine asked to see me."

Berwig's cheeks seemed to collapse. "Who told you that?" he demanded, his nose turning an even darker shade of purple.

"I did," Lucabara said.

Berwig started to say something, but checked himself. Instead, he turned to Senyous.

The old Montmer slipped forward, reached up, pulled down one of Berwig's ears and whispered directly into it.

Berwig listened. As he did his lips pursed, his cheeks bulged again, so that his eyes seemed to retreat into his face. When Senyous finished speaking Berwig stood up and looked at Lucabara. "Who," he demanded, "gave you permission to fetch this . . . Perloo?"

"Jolaine," she replied.

Berwig stood there, tongue-tied.

Senyous tugged at his smock sleeve. With a start, Berwig bent over while more words were whispered into his ear. Then he wheeled about to face Lucabara.

"Ah, yes," the granter's cub said loudly, trying to sound casual. "I almost forgot. He and my mother chatted sometimes. Well, she's not all there, is she?

"But I suppose we might as well humor her," he went on. "What was your name?" he asked Perloo.

"Perloo."

"*Per-loo*, eh?" he spoke as if he had never heard the name before. "You do know that my mother's not what she once was. So don't be too upset if she's confused you with someone else."

"I am sorry," Perloo said. "Would it be all right if I went and saw her?"

Berwig looked around. Every Montmer in the room was waiting for his answer. In haste, he beckoned Senyous to his side.

When Senyous spoke into his ear Berwig nodded again and approached Perloo.

"See Jolaine?" Berwig said, as if reciting memorized lines. "Well, I don't know why not." He put his arm around Perloo's shoulder and gave him an awkward squeeze. "Let's just hope the old biddy hasn't lost the rest of her mind while she waited for you to come. Wouldn't want that, now would we?"

So saying, he guided Perloo forcibly away. Even as he did three warriors in full armor—beckoned by Senyous—sprang forward and began to follow.

As Perloo was marched off he twisted around to look back. Those at the table were still watching in silence. Lucabara, with intense alarm, was looking after him too. But when she took a hop in his direction, Senyous deftly placed himself between her and the door, preventing her from moving.

Perloo, who wanted to tell her not to worry about him, made a motion to break away from Berwig. The big Montmer gripped him too tightly. "This way, my young pup, this way."

Perloo had no choice but to go where Berwig led.

SOME QUESTIONS

"IS JOLAINE SUFFERING a great deal?" Perloo asked as Berwig led him away.

"Suffering?" Berwig sputtered. In place of his sham smile was a hard, furious look. "She's decrepit. Useless. She's so old she can't think right."

"I'm sorry to hear it," Perloo said. "She's been a wonderful granter."

"That's what you say," Berwig said, squeezing Perloo's neck even tighter. Behind them marched the three warriors, pikes on the ready.

Perloo's previous visits to Jolaine had all taken place in her busy public rooms, high in the burrow. Though he had never seen her private chambers, he assumed they were in the same general area and that it was there Berwig was taking him. But as they continued to hop forward, taking one turn after another, it became clear to him that they were heading *down*. And no one else was there.

Suddenly, Berwig halted. Perloo, having no choice stopped too.

"Hop off!" Berwig barked to the three warriors. "I've something private to say."

The three warriors took a few hops away and folded down their ears.

Perloo waited patiently, as Berwig, laboring with his thoughts, chewed his upper lip. Not for an instant, however, did the big fellow loosen his grip.

"Look here," Berwig finally burst out, eyes more squinty than ever, "I need to know why Jolaine sent for you."

Perloo blinked his baggy eyes. "I wasn't told," he replied.

"That's a lie!" Berwig cried. "She asked you to come, didn't she?"

"Lucabara only said Jolaine asked me to visit."

Brushing aside the explanation with a wave of his paw, Berwig said, "You used to talk to Jolaine a lot. In private. Huddled together like conspirators. I want to know what it was all about."

"We enjoyed talking about mythology and history," Perloo explained.

"What *kind* of history?" Berwig demanded.

"Montmer history."

Berwig snorted with contempt. "I don't care slush for history. What I want to know—and I want to know *now*—is what else you talked about. You were the only one she spoke to like that."

"I was?"

"What did my mother say would happen when she died?"

"She didn't say anything," Perloo said. "Why would she? I'm a nobody."

"Exactly!" Berwig sneered, ears shaking with anger.

"I mean," Perloo went on, "it would have been rude to ask her such a thing. It's none of my business. Besides, I'm not even interested in politics or anything like that."

"You did ask her because—" Berwig began to say only to cut himself off. Instead, he yanked at his whisker ends even while his nose quivered—as if he could smell out what he was seeking. "What about the Felbarts?" he barked.

"The Felbarts?"

"You're stalling," Berwig screamed. "What did she say about the Felbarts?"

"We talked about old wars," Perloo said. "How she hoped we'd never have another war with them."

"Said she'd get rid of our warriors, didn't she?"

"I don't think so."

"I think the army is our best friend," Berwig bellowed, loud enough for the three warriors to hear.

"Well, actually," Perloo began, "She—"

"Never mind!" Berwig cut in. "Just tell me what she told you about her successor."

"Her *what?*"

In an outburst of frustration, Berwig kicked out with one of his long feet, striking Perloo hard across his skinny shins. Taken by surprise, Perloo fell to the ground.

"Stop acting like a worm!" Berwig barked. "I want to know what my mother said about her successor."

"Nothing," Perloo returned, rubbing the place where he'd been hit and deeply regretting having come.

"Of all the . . ." mumbled Berwig. He glanced at the warriors who had inched forward. "Stand back!" he snapped. "Bend those ears! If you want a promotion when I become granter do as you're told!"

The warriors leaped to do as ordered.

Berwig, bending over Perloo, grasped his smock at the neck and hauled him to his feet. "Are you saying that Jolaine never talked to you about what would happen after she died? Not once? *Ever?*"

Perloo, truly wishing he could provide a satisfactory answer, searched his memory. "Well, once she did tell me how she succeeded her father's place when her father chose her as tribe leader."

Berwig's nose turned crimson. "She wasn't *chosen!*" he bellowed. "She was his only cub! As I'm hers. It was *automatic.*"

"I suppose that's true," Perloo agreed, wanting more than anything to avoid arguments. He would have given a lot to be back in his snug burrow.

"When she dies," Berwig snarled, "the title comes to me. Do you understand? *Me!* What I need to know," he went on, "is if you speak to her now, what are you going to say?"

"I was just going to listen," Perloo insisted. "Really, I'm only here because Jolaine sent for me."

"Maybe it wasn't *you* she sent for."

"But I thought—"

"I don't care a flea's nose for what you think!" Berwig cried, ears shaking. "My mother is old. Out of her mind! Talks nothing but gibberish!"

"But I thought she sent for me and—"

Berwig struck another blow, kicking so hard Perloo fell back against the wall. There he slumped, legs smarting painfully.

"Put him in the middle cell," Berwig ordered. "I'll take care of him later."

The three warriors hopped forward, gathered the hapless Perloo up by his stubby arms and hauled him away down an old, dusty tunnel. The ground was littered with rubble. Walls were crumbling. The way grew narrower too, and—save for an occasional sputtering candle—darker and gloomier the farther they went.

When they did come to a halt one of the warriors yanked open a door and flung Perloo into a small, wood-paneled room. The door slammed behind him. A peg was set.

"When this door next opens," one of the warriors shouted through the door, "it'll be us, Berwig's friends. And that will be the end of you!"

PERLOO HAS SOME
THOUGHTS

STOMACH KNOTTED WITH tension, legs in pain from Berwig's kicks, Perloo lay on the wooden floor of the room. It was a small, square space. The flickering light from the sole candle stuck in the wall revealed no windows, only the one door through which he had been thrown. Opposite where he squatted a small mound of straw had been heaped. Perloo guessed it was meant to be a bed, though he supposed he could, if need be, eat some of it. When he realized that the floor, walls, and ceiling of the room were covered with tightly fitting wood paneling, Perloo had no doubt he'd been placed in a jail cell.

Creeping into a corner, he pulled up his knobby knees, rubbed his legs, smoothed his scruffy whiskers, then nestled inside his smock, pulling the top and bottom strings tightly to keep himself warm.

Searching his memory, Perloo recalled Montmers who had been killed after being thrown into jails. There had been Chillork, and Whistlepon. Notorious cases, both. There were Smerl and Jigbur too, not to mention the infamous Nopthang. It made Perloo recollect one of Mogwat's more famous sayings: "Better to live with ten Montmers in uneasy peace than fight one in a war." Berwig's threat to come back and "take care of him" filled Perloo with dread.

For a while he considered the way of Abter, who had escaped from a cell by burrowing a tunnel more than two hundred hops long. Perhaps he too might dig his way to freedom. Perloo even attempted to pry a board away from the wall so as to get to the earth behind. It was of no use. The pulling out of a board might be done with many paws, but not with two, certainly not *his* two. He was going to have to stay where he'd been put.

When hunger began to gnaw at him, Perloo halfheartedly hopped over to the straw bed and sniffed at it. It took careful searching to find a few decent stalks. Though he only nibbled, the food served to soothe him.

Back in his corner Perloo concentrated on the big puzzle. *Why* had Berwig treated him in such a fashion? One thing was clear: Berwig was nervous about his succession to the position of granter. Why that should be so was beyond anything Perloo could guess.

But as Perloo squatted there—staring at the blank walls of his jail cell—he recollected one particular discussion with Jolaine. The two had been chatting about the history of Montmer leadership. She mentioned that in earlier times leadership almost always went to the eldest of the granter's cubs. Almost, *not* always. A dying leader could name *any* Montmer who was in good standing to be the next granter.

Perloo had been so surprised by this claim he checked his library to see if it was true. Jolaine was right. Over the course of tribal history seven dying granters had selected someone other than their own cubs to be the new granter.

Perhaps, Perloo mused, it was his knowledge of such times—when the successor to a dying granter had *not* been automatic—that so alarmed Berwig. But surely others knew about these precedents. Was Berwig going to put all Montmers who knew their history in prison?

Even so, when he asked himself who else might know their history he couldn't think of any. That made him recall Mogwat's saying that, "Too often a Montmer will take one today over three yesterdays and two tomorrows."

The more Perloo thought about it, the more a new idea blossomed in his mind. Perhaps Jolaine—on her deathbed—was going to proclaim someone *other* than Berwig to succeed her!

Suddenly—like an avalanche—Perloo knew what was going to happen. *Berwig was going to be put aside. He would not become granter.* Rare as such an event might be, it was possible.

Perloo grinned. Oh, the wonders of history! If you knew the past you could predict the future. If it had happened, it could happen again! What had Mogwat said? "The future begins in the past."

Perloo tried to guess whom Jolaine might select

for the new granter. Knowing nothing of tribal politics, he could come up with no names. It could be any one of five thousand Montmers who lived about Rasquich Mountain. Besides, as far as Perloo was concerned, to compare his own day with the illustrious past was to reveal how dull and unheroic his own time was. What better example could there be than Berwig?

"Oh, dry dust. What does it matter?" Perloo sighed, the excitement of discovery evaporating. Berwig had him, and wanted to get rid of him. His only chance was to stay awake and resist.

Perloo, however, was exhausted. Though he tried to keep from sleeping, the gloominess of the cell, its utter stillness, and dwindling light proved too much for his resolution. He soon fell asleep.

How long he slept Perloo never knew. When he woke it was with a start. The candle in the room had gutted. The cell was dark and cold, but his ears had caught the sound of someone opening the door.

"It's Berwig!" a frightened Perloo whispered to himself. "He's come back to kill me."

A VISITOR

A TERRIFIED PERLOO gazed at the door, trying desperately to recall what the ancient heroes he'd read so much about had done when confronted by a challenge. The best response he could recall was Buxabec the Brave's speech at the Battle of Liggin's Creek, during the Ninth Montmer–Felbart War.

"Friends," Buxabec had said to his warriors when he had accepted the traditional challenge from the Felbarts, "sometimes there's nothing to do but square your feet and fight!"

"Square your feet. Square your feet," Perloo kept saying to himself as he attempted to keep his long feet in a fighting stance.

Body trembling, breathing labored, continually brushing back his whiskers in agitation, Perloo faced the door. "Oh, Mogwat, give my legs strength. Please!"

The door swung open.

"Perloo?" a voice called. "Are you here?" Around the door—illuminated by a candle—appeared the face of Lucabara, her long ears cocked, her blue nose sniffing.

"Lucabara!" Perloo cried, all but swooning in relief. "Thank Mogwat it's you!"

Lucabara hopped into the room and shut the door quickly. "Are you all right?" she asked, holding up her candle.

"Well, yes, I think I am," Perloo replied, heart still hammering and all but faint with relief. "A little . . . frightened . . . but, perfectly fine. How did you know to look for me?"

"When I saw those three armed warriors follow you and Berwig from the Great Hall I became worried," Lucabara explained. "I tried to follow, but Senyous wouldn't let me go with you."

"Who's Senyous?"

"Oh, Perloo, don't you know *anybody*?"

"I guess not."

"Senyous was that small, stooped fellow who kept giving Berwig advice. 'Senyous the Sly' he's called. And he's vicious. Anyway, when Berwig returned to the hall without you, looking very smug, I decided I'd better find you.

"First I checked Jolaine's room. When I learned you never got there I knew something was wrong. Tell me what happened."

"It's Berwig," Perloo said. "He kept asking me about my talks with Jolaine. He's nervous about his succession to granter. But Lucabara, I don't care about any of that. I just want to go home. You've got to help me."

"Perloo," she replied, "you must see Jolaine first."

Perloo shook his head. "No. Absolutely not. It's too much. All I want is to go home."

Lucabara lifted her candle and scrutinized Perloo with a look of scorn. What she said, however, was, "They didn't leave a warrior on guard. Good thing, or I would never have been able to come. I guess they thought you'd just stay put."

She poked her head out of the cell door. "No one's around," she called. "Follow me."

In three hops Perloo was out of the cell and in a dark, muddy passageway. "Which way?" he asked.

"That way leads to the Great Hall," Lucabara said, pointing. "We better go the other direction."

As they hopped along, Perloo said, "How did you know I was in that jail?"

"There are only three prison cells in the burrow. They're all in a row. I tried the others first. Not that they've been used much. Not till lately."

Perloo halted. "What do you mean, 'Not till lately'?"

"Senyous is using them for other prisoners."

"Is this Senyous in charge of things?"

"More and more."

They hopped on past what seemed to Perloo an endless number of empty passageways and storerooms. Some rooms were empty. Others were filled with food, candles, or pelts. "You do know your way around here, don't you?" he said in admiration.

"I live here," Lucabara reminded him. "Perloo, tell me *exactly* what Berwig said? It may be important."

"It seems that he—"

"Shhh!" she suddenly said, holding up a paw in warning. Her nose was quivering rapidly. From the way her ears shook, Perloo was sure she had caught some troubling sound.

He listened and heard it too: the sound of hopping, enough to suggest many feet.

"I was just in time," Lucabara said in a hushed voice. "They're coming for you."

Perloo's stomach churned. "Lucabara," he said, "please get me out of here!"

"Follow me!" She began to bounce quickly down a tunnel. Perloo, constantly looking back over his shoulder, followed. After twenty hops Lucabara took a sharp turn.

Just as he was going around the corner, Perloo heard a commotion in the direction from which they'd just come. In spite of himself he stopped and listened.

"He's gone!" came a shout. "Escaped!"

It was Berwig's voice.

"Treason! Conspiracy! Rebellion!" he cried. "Find the traitor! Don't let him get away! Alarm! Treason!" As Berwig's words were taken up, the sound of hops multiplied.

Perloo felt his arm jerked. "Come on!" Lucabara cried. "They move fast."

Panicky, Perloo moved twice as fast as before, great bounding leaps that covered three normal hops at a time.

"In here," Lucabara cried. Gasping for breath, Perloo followed her into a tiny, dark, foul smelling room. Lucabara pulled the door shut behind them.

"Where are we?" Perloo asked, holding his nose.

"They grow mushrooms here."

"Lucabara, all I want is to get out and—"

"Stop thinking only about yourself!" Lucabara snapped. "And be quiet!"

Mortified, Perloo clenched his teeth and listened.

The sound of hops came from outside the little room. "Half of you go that way," a small, reedy voice piped. "The rest go the other direction. Find Perloo fast. He mustn't reach Jolaine or get out of the burrow. If you have to kill him to hold him, do it!"

There were murmurs of "Yes, Senyous," "Don't worry, Senyous," "We'll get him." This was followed by more hops, then silence.

Perloo leaned against a wall. Tears trickled down his cheeks, flowed along his whiskers, and dripped down to the ground.

"I think they're gone," Lucabara whispered.

"Lucabara," Perloo said, "why do Berwig and Senyous hate me so much? If they knew anything about me they'd know I'd rather stay home with my books."

"Perloo," Lucabara returned, "you *still* don't understand what's happening, do you?"

"All I know is this," Perloo said, and repeated his conversation with Berwig in as much detail as he could.

Lucabara listened intently.

"Does that make any sense to you?" Perloo asked when he'd finished.

Lucabara's only reply was, "You must see Jolaine."

"No!" Perloo snapped, balling his paws up into fists. "How many times do I have to say it: *I don't want to be involved*. I'm nothing. A nobody. A mistake! Just get me outside. I'll ski home so fast I'll be nothing but a blur!"

"Is that what you truly want?" Lucabara demanded. "No challenges?"

"Exactly," Perloo returned. "A quiet, simple life of reading and thinking. No fuss. No bother. No politics."

"No life," Lucabara added.

"Lucabara, you don't understand. I can read about heroes. I'm no good at being one."

Lucabara studied him pensively. Then she said, "Fine. I know some secret doors and passageways. Just be quiet and do exactly what I tell you."

"Thank you," returned Perloo, relieved that she was finally accepting who he was.

Lucabara opened the door of the room and peeked out. "Come on. It's safe."

The two hopped along the tunnel, their feet making soft, flop, flop, flop sounds as they went. Now and again Lucabara paused. From the way her long ears twitched, Perloo could tell she was listening intently. He listened too as well as sniffed, but caught no hint of danger.

They reached what appeared to be the very bottom of the burrow. The air was damp, the floor oozing with slime and mud. Cobwebs, guarded by fat spiders, draped from ceilings. Odd-shaped fungi grew everywhere. Walls bore ancient pictographs, faded depictions of ancient Montmers.

Lucabara guided them to a small side tunnel. "We'll have to crawl," she warned.

Perloo, eying the narrow passage and the mud, rubbed his paws nervously. "How far are we from the outside?"

"Just follow me."

Lucabara got down on her knees, lowered her ears, and began to crawl through the tunnel. Perloo, muttering complaints, did the same. At the end of the tunnel they entered a small, round room high enough for them to stand. In the center was a ladder.

"Someone sure wanted to make it hard to get outside," Perloo said, gazing up but unable to see the top. "Will this get me there?" he wondered out loud.

Instead of replying Lucabara began to climb. Perloo followed.

It was not easy. Their long feet required them to climb with backs to the ladder, using their heels to step up the rungs.

When they reached the top—Perloo was quite sure they had gone from the bottom of the burrow to the top—they hopped into a small alcove, empty save for a latched door on one wall.

"Does *that* lead outside?" Perloo asked hopefully.

"Go through and you'll see," she said.

"Won't it be guarded?" Perloo asked.

"I'll check," she said.

Lucabara poked her head beyond then pulled back. "No warriors," she announced.

Perloo pulled his whiskers and rubbed his paws. "Lucabara," he murmured, "thank you for your help. I'm sorry about not seeing Jolaine. Please don't think poorly of me. Really, I wouldn't be of much help. And I . . . I'm no good at speeches."

"Just go though that door," Lucabara urged.

With a guilt equal to his great relief, Perloo braced himself, then passed through the door.

But instead of stepping into the storm he found himself in yet another room. It was a shadowy place, the air thick with fumes and smoke from pots of burning incense. A few candles provided murky light.

Blinking his baggy eyes, Perloo peered through the gloom. Gradually, he made out a high moss bed in the center of the room. On the bed, propped against a bundle of dry grass, looking as frail as an old bird, lay Granter Jolaine.

JOLAINE THE GOOD

GRANTER JOLAINE'S GRAY face was withered. Her breathing was slow and irregular, with a hint of painful rattle. Her small nose—green with age —quivered feebly. Her neck tuft, white as snow and thin as gossamer, was wrapped about her neck like a scarf. Her long feet, swathed in marmot fur, stuck up at the end of the bed. Dressed in a smock of blue ermine, her thin arms lay atop a woven grass comforter. Her paws clutched a small book: *The Adventures of Mogwat the Magpie*.

Whirling about, Perloo took a hop toward the little door.

Lucabara blocked his way. "I've locked the door," she said. "Do your duty." She pointed in the direction of the dying granter. "Go to her."

"But . . ."

"For Mogwat's sake, Perloo," Lucabara cried, "*go!*"

Perloo hopped timidly toward the bed. As he drew close, Jolaine moved her head. With lidded eyes, she peered in his direction.

"Who's there?" she asked in a voice as soft as a passing cloud.

"It's me, Granter, Perloo," he said pulling down his left ear and holding it in his trembling paws.

The old Montmer worked her thin lips into a smile. "Perloo," she said, "how generous of you to come."

Feeling a stab of shame at his reluctance to visit, Perloo rubbed his paws and fussed with his whiskers. "I'm . . . I'm sorry you're so ill," he murmured.

Jolaine lifted a limp paw from her book only to let it drop. "Merely old," she said. "Perloo, there's no time . . . for pleasantries. Draw closer. Listen with care."

"I'm listening, Granter."

"Your paw," she said, holding out one of hers. Perloo obeyed. Jolaine wrapped her four fingers— thin as snowberry stalks—around Perloo's, giving them a delicate squeeze.

"I am dying," she began.

Perloo lifted a paw in protest.

"Don't talk. Just listen. Perloo, you and I have chatted about old ways. You, next to myself, know more Montmer history than anyone else. You know our tribal laws. Our traditions. You know the way we've changed. In olden times we granters . . . had absolute authority. But our tribe has now moved toward newer freedoms. We must not regress. As Mogwat said"— Jolaine squeezed the book she was holding—"'When you take one backward hop . . . it requires two hops to go forward.' Perloo, Montmers *must* go forward. They need to live in greater freedom."

Jolaine closed her eyes. Her speech had taken much effort. Perloo waited patiently until she spoke again.

"Perloo, are you still here?"

"Yes, Granter."

"Good. My only cub, Berwig, would make a bad granter," she continued. "As Mogwat has told us, 'Fear not the weak, only they who try to hide their weaknesses.' Berwig is weak. Lazy. Insensitive. Senyous, his friend, is treacherous. Neither can be trusted."

The old Montmer breathed deeply. The rattle grew more pronounced.

"Over most of our . . . history," she went on, "the eldest cub of the passing granter became the new granter. But as you know, Perloo . . . not always. It is my responsibility to select another."

Jolaine, summoning strength again, paused. When she opened her eyes she gazed at him. "Perloo," she said at last, "my choice to be the next granter is . . . you."

"*Me?*" Perloo said with a gasp, staring wide-eyed at Jolaine.

The old Montmer managed a smile. "Yes, Perloo, you are to be . . . the next granter."

A dumbfounded Perloo glanced at Lucabara to make sure he had heard correctly. She gave him a nod as much to say, "Yes, it's true."

Perloo turned back to Jolaine. "But . . . but," he stammered, "how could I be? I'm nothing!"

"You are Perloo," Jolaine whispered. "Learned but modest. You have your weaknesses . . . but you don't hide them.

"Among all Montmers, you know more of our history than any other. That will enable you to be true to yourself."

Jolaine paused and closed her eyes. Her energy was ebbing fast.

"But I don't even want to be granter!" Perloo blurted out. "I want to stay in my burrow and read."

The old granter snorted softly. "That's not weakness. It's wisdom."

"It's a weakness to others!" Perloo cried.

"Perloo," Jolaine said, "you cannot have the luxury of doing what you wish. I am about to proclaim you my successor."

"Don't I have any say in the matter?" Perloo implored, eyes full of tears.

Jolaine's face clouded. Her body tensed. "It's Berwig. He wishes to turn from our progress. To hop backward. To become a dictator. I fear he intends to make a new war against the Felbarts."

"*War!*" Perloo recoiled with horror. "Is there any reason for a war?"

"None. But I think that's his, and . . . Senyous's plan. They have been building up the army. Making promises to warriors."

"But how can *I* stop them? Even if I know a lot that doesn't mean I can *do* anything!"

"Lucabara," Jolaine called in a whisper. "Bring me the . . . proclamation."

Lucabara hopped to a box that stood at the foot of Jolaine's bed. From it she removed a bark scroll six paws in length and width, kept rolled up by a twist of kinnikinnik.

"Untie it," the old Montmer requested in an ever diminishing voice.

With a soft flutter, the scroll opened.

"Perloo," Jolaine said, "read this for yourself." She held out the sheet of bark.

Reluctantly, Perloo took the sheet and glanced at the words. The room was too dim and Perloo too dazed to focus clearly so he only pretended to read the document before returning it to Jolaine.

Jolaine pressed it to her chest. "There," she whispered, "do you understand all I have said?"

"I . . . think so," Perloo said softly.

"My paw is proof," Jolaine continued. "So, above all else, protect this."

"We will," Lucabara said from across the room.

"Good," Jolaine said. "Now, Perloo—Perloo the Unwilling—hold your left ear with your right paw."

"But . . ."

"Do as your granter bids," Jolaine said with a touch of her old authority. "Now, Perloo," the granter continued, "do you promise to maintain and enlarge the freedoms of all Montmers?"

"Please, can't I just—"

"*Perloo*," Lucabara pleaded from across the bed. "She's fading."

"Yes or no?" Jolaine asked.

"Well . . ." Perloo managed to say, "I suppose . . . oh, bird's teeth . . . but . . . oh, well . . . *yes!*"

"All Montmers thank you," Jolaine said in a small voice. Ears drooping, face pale, eyes closed, the old granter lay back upon her grass pillow. "Granter Perloo, before me and the witness . . . Lucabara, you have made a promise to which you are bound. Lucabara, fetch me a marking stick. I must sign the . . . proclamation. Hurry. . . . I am . . . going."

Lucabara dropped the scroll on the bed then hopped back to the chest and brought out a marking stick.

Even as she did there came a great thump on the room's main door. "Let me in!" a voice demanded. It was Berwig.

THE PROCLAMATION

CHAPTER 8

NOW THOROUGHLY frightened, Perloo turned to face the door.

"Let me in!" Berwig demanded.

"Hurry," Jolaine urged. "I must sign the proclamation!"

Lucabara hopped to a burning candle, put the tip of a marking stick into the flame, charred it black, then jumped back and offered it to Jolaine.

"Open the door!" Berwig cried. "Immediately!"

"Keep him out!" Jolaine whispered.

Perloo—too rattled to think—was standing with his mouth agape. Jolaine's order startled him into action. He hopped forward, only to trip over his own feet and go crashing against the door, fortunately blocking it.

"Treason!" Berwig shouted from outside. "Conspiracy! Save the granter! My mother is in danger! Find Senyous! Break the door in!"

Jolaine took up the marking stick in her weak paws as Lucabara spread the scroll so she could sign it.

"Open up!" Berwig screamed. The door shook violently.

Perloo struggled to his feet and pressed his paws against the door even as he looked frantically back over his shoulder.

"I don't have . . . enough strength," Jolaine whispered to Lucabara. "Guide my . . ."

Lucabara—glancing at Perloo—leaned forward and placed one of her paws over Jolaine's

With a loud snap, one of the door panels burst. Perloo tried to push it back, but could not. A paw reached through and attempted to grab something. Not knowing what else to do, Perloo bit it.

"Ow!" came a cry. The paw jerked back.

Jolaine—with Lucabara's help—started to sign her name. Halfway through the signature the soot on the marking stick gave out. Lucabara leaped to put the tip into the flame again.

As the banging and shoving on the door increased, a second panel split. This time two paws reached in and groped. Perloo hopped away, searching for something—anything—to beat back the intruders.

Finding nothing, he hopped to the side of the bed just in time to see Jolaine complete the laborious process of writing her name.

The signing had taken her remaining energy. With a murmur that was half sigh, half groan, she dropped the marking stick and fell back upon her pillows.

"Lucabara . . ." Jolaine cried, letting forth with a

long thin squeak of a breath. It was as if a frail limb on an old tree was breaking. With a snap, the proclamation scroll rolled itself back up.

A third panel on the door smashed open. Many paws reached in, trying to locate the latch that held the door shut.

Lucabara looked across the bed at Perloo. "Jolaine's dead!" she whispered in awe.

Perloo, who could think of nothing but escaping, peered through the smoky haze. There was the small doorway through which he and Lucabara had entered. "The alcove!" he cried and sprang forward. It would not open. Lucabara had locked it. Perloo spun about. Lucabara, overcome with grief, had remained standing by the bed, staring at the dead granter.

In two hops Perloo returned to her side, grabbed her arm, and began to drag her toward the alcove door. "Unlock it!" he shouted.

"The proclamation!" she cried.

Even as she spoke the main door to the room exploded inward. Berwig's bulky body filled the door frame. Peering around from behind him were a host of armed warriors.

Lucabara, seeing Berwig, gave a yelp. With a yank, she pulled herself free of Perloo's grip, returned to Jolaine's side, snatched up the scroll, then bounded back toward Perloo. He was trying desperately to open the alcove door.

Berwig took one look at Jolaine and realized she

had died. "Dead!" he bellowed. "My mother is dead!"

He turned to Lucabara. Even as he did she tried to hide the scroll behind her back. Suspicions instantly aroused, Berwig lunged forward and tried to grab it, but only managed to grasp hold of one end.

For a brief moment Lucabara and Berwig both held the proclamation. But Berwig, being bigger and stronger, began to haul it in.

Seeing the danger, remembering Jolaine's words that he must protect the proclamation above all else, Perloo grabbed hold of Lucabara and pulled with her. For a moment all was in balance until, with a re-sounding rip, the scroll split in two.

Tumbling backward, Berwig collided into his war-riors, mowing them down like so many dandelions in a storm.

Simultaneously, Lucabara and Perloo careened in the opposite direction, snapping the lock on the al-cove door, and tumbling into the little room.

"Stop them!" Berwig bellowed, floundering midst his warriors as he tried to get to his feet. "Arrest them! I am the granter! Stop them!"

Perloo slammed the alcove door shut and latched it from the inside. "Do you have the proclamation?" he cried.

"Just part of it!" Lucabara sobbed in dismay. The little door was being pounded upon.

"We have to go," Perloo cried and sprang toward the ladder. He began to go down only to realize that

Lucabara was not coming. Fearful of what a furious Berwig might do to her, and she too distraught to think clearly, Perloo scrambled back up. Sure enough, Lucabara, still in shock, was simply standing there.

"Lucabara!" Perloo urged. "Hurry!"

"I can't leave her," she sobbed.

"Jolaine is dead!" Perloo cried. "We've got to save ourselves." Once more he started down. After a few rungs he stopped. "What am I saying!" he said to himself. "What am I doing? Don't I have any feelings? Great Mogwat, Jolaine is dead! This is awful!" He looked up. To his great relief Lucabara was coming.

"Lucabara . . ." he started to say.

"Go!" she cried.

The two—almost tumbling in their haste—worked their way down. When they reached the bottom an abashed Perloo said, "Lucabara, please, forgive me. I didn't mean to be so unfeeling. I'm all confused. I'm all . . ."

"Granter Jolaine died," Lucabara whispered.

"I know she has," Perloo replied. "And—oh, bird's teeth—it *is* awful. Terrible awful. But . . . but, we can't stay here."

"You're the new granter," Lucabara said to him.

"No!" Perloo yelped. "I'm just Perloo. But they'll be after me anyway. I know they will. You have to help me get out of here!"

Lucabara held up the piece of proclamation that Jolaine had signed. "It's not even all here," she said.

Whereas I, Granter Jolaine,
in the noble line of Tornagerty
come to the end of my life,

And whereas, I, Granter Jolaine,
Mountain tribe to go forward
freedom:

And whereas, my only cub Berwig,
on restoring old, absolutist ways, and
take back the old Granter power

And whereas, I, Granter Jolaine,
by ancient law to pr
as Granter,

I, Granter Jolaine, hereby proclaim
my successor with all the
Granter, with the hope a
will preserve and enlarge
Montmer.

Jo

"Without the other half," Lucabara said with dismay, "this is meaningless."

"For Mogwat's sake, Lucabara!" Perloo pleaded. "Take it with you. We'll deal with it later."

Lucabara continued to stare at the torn piece of proclamation.

"They must have gone down there!" came a voice from high over their heads. "After them, toadstools!" There was a clatter as warriors started down the ladder.

It was enough to jolt Lucabara from her shock. She blinked, wiggled her nose—the smell of their pursuers was not only strong but offensive—stuffed the proclamation half into her smock, and began to crawl through the small tunnel.

Perloo scrambled after her.

BERWIG ACTS

BY THE TIME Berwig and his warriors reached the bottom of the ladder, Perloo and Lucabara had disappeared through the small tunnel.

Berwig squinted at the small hole. One look and he knew it would be hard to squeeze his bulk through. He did not even want to try. Instead he shouted orders. "Seal all the doors to the outside! Post armed warriors at every exit and each passageway! Carry your pikes! Make sure they're sharp! Show no mercy! Hurry! Perloo mustn't get out!"

As the warriors hopped away—some back up the ladder, others through the narrow tunnel—Berwig returned to Jolaine's room.

The room was dark and very quiet, fragrant with the residue of the sweet-smelling herbs. Standing before the bed, Berwig's fat ears twitched, his nose quivered, the tips of his toes trembled. Though it was his mother who lay dead before him, he was consumed only by feelings of betrayal. All he could think was: *She would not allow me to become granter.*

From the time of his infancy—when he first understood what the position of *granter* meant—Berwig had assumed the title would be his. As he saw it, the position was his by right of birth. As he grew older his longing to be granter became an obsession. He thought of little else. As his mother aged, he became impatient to claim the title.

Then, as Jolaine's age and illness could no longer be denied, she informed her only cub that she had made up her mind: He would *not* be granter.

"But why?" Berwig demanded.

"You're not fit to be a leader."

"If I'm not, it's your fault," he sulked. "You're my mother. It was your responsibility to make me right."

She replied by quoting Mogwat. "Life is given. The rest one gives oneself."

At first Berwig thought she was teasing. But gradually he grasped that his mother was in earnest. His reaction was outrage. How dare she even suggest that he was not good enough to become granter! The title was his birthright!

He apologized, argued, insisted, threatened, wept, made promise after promise. She would not change her mind.

Rage was followed by fear that others would hear of her decision. He would be mocked. Ridiculed. Humiliated.

Then Jolaine informed him that she had chosen Perloo to succeed her.

"Perloo?" Berwig cried. "Who's he?"

"The one with whom I talk history," Jolaine informed him.

"He's a nobody!" Berwig ranted. "Nothing but a book reader!"

Jolaine would not change her mind.

"Does this Perloo know what you're intending to do?" Berwig asked.

"He will know when he needs to know," Jolaine replied.

In desperation, Berwig turned to Senyous for guidance. Senyous had been first assistant to Jolaine's father. As a courtesy she had kept him on. When it became clear he was bent on securing power for himself, she dismissed him.

When Berwig asked Senyous for advice, the old retainer relished the notion of helping the rejected son conspire to take over the grantership. Fulsome in his flattery, Senyous encouraged Berwig to think the grantership was his for the taking. The two planned and schemed.

And now . . .

Berwig unfolded the half piece of the proclamation that he had torn from Lucabara's grasp. Squinting in the gloom he read it.

sixty-third Granter
the First, have

wish the Montmer
in the pursuit of

appears bent
seeks to
unto himself:

have the right,
oclaim anyone in the Tribe

Perloo to be
rights and privileges of
nd expectation that he
the freedom of every

LAINE

Though Berwig read it through three times he could make no sense of it, except that it probably would not help his cause.

Full of fury and frustration, Berwig stuffed the proclamation into his smock. "By Mogwat," he cried aloud at his mother's body, "I will be granter!"

Then he made himself think. Senyous's advice had been clear. As soon as Jolaine died, he, Berwig, must sit upon the Settop, proclaim himself granter and then hold on to the title in any way he could. That moment had arrived. With thumping heart and shaking knees he quit Jolaine's room and hopped toward the Great Hall.

Suddenly he stopped. What about Perloo? And Lucabara. Should he or should he not say something about them?

"I'll say Perloo murdered Jolaine," Berwig decided in haste. "As for Lucabara, I won't even mention her. She's too popular."

When Berwig reached the entryway to the Great Hall he paused. He felt weak. Frightened. A saying of Mogwat's fluttered through his mind. "Lies fly then fall. Truth hops but keeps going."

What would he do if the tribe rejected him? Just thinking about it made him feel ill.

Twice Berwig backed away from the door. Twice —because his fear of retreat was equal to his fear of going forward—he returned. He had to keep reminding himself that this was the moment he must seize.

Berwig tried to make himself look as if he were suffering. He ruffled his dyed whiskers, bent his ears, pinched his cheeks till they turned white, loosened his smock strings to suggest inner disorder. Finally, he bowed his head, touched a paw to his heart, and began to breathe deeply.

When Berwig entered the hall a goodly number of

Montmers were about. The mood was solemn and tense. Some were squatting by the warm fires. Others were munching away at bowls. Most were talking in low voices. Although news of Granter Jolaine's death had not been announced, everyone in the Central Tribe Burrow knew of her grave condition.

Berwig fixed a gloomy look upon his face and moved with heavy hops toward the Settop. Close to the stone bench he paused and stood motionless. Massive back to the crowd, he gazed upon the throne mournfully. Though most of his strength was taken up by the effort to keep his shaking knees still, he kept darting squinty-eyed looks over his shoulder to see if anyone was paying attention to him.

Gradually, Berwig's manner began to draw attention. When he continued to stand before the Settop, eyes closed, breathing deeply, paws clenching and unclenching, uttering deep, lugubrious sighs, it became apparent to the onlookers that something momentous had occurred. A hush descended upon the hall.

Berwig turned. With a theatrical start of surprise that he was being observed, he swallowed once, twice, and wiped an eye, as if to brush away a tear. In a heavy, breaking voice he stammered, "Much loved . . . Montmers . . . I have . . . shocking . . . news to share with you." His heart was throbbing so with fear of rejection he was sure he was going to pass out. Gasping with pain, puffing out his cheeks, he forced himself to

speak. "My mother," he began, "Granter Jolaine—
Jolaine the Good—has been—*murdered*!"

A gasp of horror rippled through the crowd.

"Murdered," Berwig continued in a voice squeak-
ing with nervousness, "by a traitor who seeks to take
the power and authority of granter!"

"Oh!" the crowd moaned, moved by Berwig's dis-
play of emotion.

Speaking louder, Berwig went on, "I have lost . . .
not just a beloved mother . . . and my dearest friend,
but . . . our cherished leader. It is in her name that I,
Berwig the Big, hereditary granter, heir obvious, vow
vengeance upon those who have taken her from us so
cruelly."

With elaborate gestures—all the while gulping
painfully for breath—he smoothed his smock behind
him, tugged at his sleeves, brushed away a few more
pretend tears—then laboriously lowered himself
upon the Settop.

Berwig's seating himself was fully understood by
the crowd of onlookers. Ears twitched. Noses quivered. There were gasps, moans, sniffles. A few whispered, "Oh, my!" "How sad!" "What an end!" "Poor
Jolaine." Most, however, simply stared at Berwig in
stunned silence.

Having seated himself—almost swooning with excitement and fright in the process—Berwig covered
his eyes with his paws and swallowed great drafts
of air.

So far so good. No one had denounced him. No one had mocked him. Stealthily, he spread his claws over his face and peaked out to see the reaction of the crowd, ready to flee if there was so much as a flicker of opposition. Not one objection was raised. Not an ill word was spoken. The Great Hall was still.

Berwig remained sitting, paws upon fat knees, long feet before him, toes wiggling with the sheer excitement and thrill of his position. Unable to suppress his glee, he suddenly grinned a full expanse of gap teeth, flung out his arms and croaked, "Look at me! I'm granter! *Me!*" When he began to snort he slapped a paw over his mouth to suppress it.

The crowd knew what was expected of them. They reached up and—more in sorrow than submission—saluted Berwig by pulling their left ears down.

The salute caused Berwig to grin though he was quick to smother it with a series of solemn grunts, which he hoped would be taken as an acknowledgment of the homage paid.

"Hear me, my subjects," he cried. "The name of the traitor is already known. It is—Perloo!"

There was scratching of ears and exchanged looks of puzzlement. "Who is Perloo?" was heard.

"Even as we speak," Berwig continued, growing stronger and more confident with every passing moment that no one objected, "my warriors are searching for him. All Montmers are welcome—indeed encouraged, urged, required—to help in the search.

Whoever catches the traitor shall . . ." Berwig searched his thoughts for a rich reward. "They shall have . . . my . . . gratitude!" he cried out.

"On the other paw," Berwig went on, "anyone aiding or abetting the traitor shall be treated as part of this ghastly conspiracy. No mercy shall be shown. None!

"Now," Berwig hurried to say before the crowd could do or say anything, "there will be two weeks of mourning for my mother, the late, beloved Granter Jolaine the Good. After such time I shall have my proper installation as granter with the pageantry all Montmers love so well.

"But," he pressed on, speaking faster as he gained confidence, "to make sure there is no confusion among Montmers and to maintain order and decorum at this moment of grave crisis, I hereby suspend all freedoms and liberties because I, Berwig, Berwig the Big," he fairly shouted, "I alone am the tribe!"

The large Montmer sat straight upon the Settop, brushed back his whiskers and gazed with squinty eyes about the room to see if anyone dared to object. But the abrupt, horrible news of Jolaine's death, followed by Berwig's pronouncements and decrees, had come so quickly the crowd was cowed. Not a word of objection was expressed.

Then, from somewhere in the Great Hall a thin, reed-like voice cried, "Well done, Berwig! Well done!"

The call rang out with such solitary shrillness that

Berwig was taken aback. "Who . . . who said that?" he demanded, prepared to bolt if any meaningful opposition was voiced.

"I did," came the reply.

The nervous crowd hopped away. In the middle of the hall stood Senyous, Senyous the Sly.

SENYOUS THE SLY

CHAPTER 10

A GRINNING, LIMPING Senyous hopped forward. As he approached Berwig he reached for his ear
—his right one—recalled himself, smirked, and duti-
fully pulled down his left ear.

"Berwig," Senyous said in a thin, reedy voice that
sounded as if a feather was caught in his throat, "may
I humbly wish you a long and happy grantership."

"I accept," Berwig replied, struggling to hold back
his immense glee.

The next moment all of Berwig's suppressed tension erupted with a ghastly itchiness that covered his
body. It was as if he had been attacked by a million
ants, each of whose tiny feet picked, poked, pinched,
and tickled as they crawled about. How he wanted to
scratch! But to scratch himself while sitting on the
Settop would not be dignified.

Unable to bear it, he sprang up and hopped out of
the room. Just as he was leaving he said, "Senyous, you
may see me in my private room."

To Berwig's back, Senyous pulled his ear again—

his right one this time—and grimaced silently. Those near him backed away.

No sooner did Berwig leave the Great Hall than he began a frenzied scratching, whimpering with relief. The next moment he began to tremble with excitement. He had won! He had sat upon the Settop! He had issued decrees! Not *one* objection had been made! Everything that Senyous had told him to do he'd done and done well! He was the sole leader! *He was granter at last!*

With a start, Berwig reminded himself that his situation was precarious. How easily his success could become undone! Perloo was free. What if someone found the other half of Jolaine's proclamation? He clutched his portion.

Then too, as far as Berwig was concerned, Senyous had not displayed proper respect toward him in the Great Hall. He, Berwig, was granter now. He must show him who was in charge. Berwig would do what *he* wanted. Without advice.

All these thoughts made his itching worse. Feeling desperate, he hopped to his private room, slamming doors behind him.

Berwig's room was set high in the burrow. Though large, it felt cramped and dirty, smelling of moldy food and unwashed feet.

As he plopped down onto his rumpled bed, an image of his mother, Jolaine, filled his mind. Briefly, Berwig was consumed by remorse and grief. He pushed it all away, thinking, *that kind of emotion mustn't be seen. She treated me badly.*

From his smock he drew out the piece of Jolaine's proclamation and studied it. Though he could make no sense of it, every instinct informed him it would not help his cause and he should rip it to shreds. He was just about to do so when there was a soft rapping on his door.

He jumped with alarm. What if Perloo was not as unknown as he had supposed? What if he had supporters? Berwig sniffed frantically. He smelled something dry, and brittle, like old, moldy leaves: Senyous.

Shoving the piece of proclamation behind his back, Berwig called, "Enter!" and drew himself up so as to look regal. What he achieved was a sticky, self-conscious grin.

Senyous slipped into the room. Delicately shutting the door behind him with a nudge of a foot, he hopped forward noiselessly.

The two Montmers looked at one another.

"Ah, Berwig," Senyous finally said in his thin, feathery voice, "how long have we planned for this moment? Our hopes. Our dreams. We are granter at last!"

"What," Berwig scowled in a low, sulky voice, "do you mean by *we*, Senyous? I am granter! Me, alone!"

"But I thought—"

"Never mind what you thought, Senyous," Berwig snapped. "I'll do my own thinking from now on!"

Shocked, Senyous scrutinized Berwig's smirking face. "Ah . . . yes," Senyous finally whispered and slowly reached up and hauled down his left ear. "You are—right. This is *your* victory. I had nothing to do with it." The old Montmer bowed so deeply his ears scraped the floor.

"That's more like it," Berwig mumbled. So saying, he scratched himself then scooped up some honey and reamed it into his mouth with both paws. Honey dribbled down his chin and onto his smock.

"Tell me, Berwig," Senyous said, "How—"

"The name, Senyous," Berwig snarled, "is *Granter* Berwig."

Senyous grimaced. "Oh, Great Granter, you are right. I need to remember that now you are high and I am low."

"Excellent," Berwig grunted.

"But," Senyous continued, "with your kind permission, oh, wise Granter, what has happened? Was Jolaine truly *murdered*?"

"I said so, didn't I?" Berwig answered.

"Yes, of course. But . . . by whom?"

"Whom do you think? Me?"

"In your presence, oh, Great Granter," Senyous intoned, "I do not think but merely react. But, may I ask, did Jolaine—before she was *murdered*, that is—do what she threatened to do, that is, proclaim someone else to be granter?"

Berwig thought for a moment then said, "I never *heard* her proclaim anyone."

Senyous cocked his head. "Never *heard* . . . I suppose there are other ways of proclaiming things. What, for instance, is that piece of bark you are holding behind the exulted broadness of your back?"

Nose turning purple, Berwig drew his paw and the half of the proclamation out from behind his back.

The old Montmer took the sheet into his shriveled paws and read it twice. He looked up. "Where's the rest of it?"

"Ah . . . I suppose Lucabara has it."

"Lucabara! Was she involved in this?"

"I . . . tore it from her hands."

"Was Perloo there?"

Berwig nodded.

"Not good," Senyous muttered. "The tribe thinks well of her. Was she, perchance, the . . . murderer?"

Berwig thought. "No," he said, "Perloo was."

"Good!"

Berwig nodded toward the torn proclamation. "Can you make anything of that?" he asked.

"Well, oh, Great Granter, I believe I could make any number of things of it—depending, oh, Granter, on what you—who are so intelligent—wish it to say."

Berwig, his itching growing worse, squinted at Senyous.

"For instance," Senyous prompted, "it might well say that your dear mother selected Perloo as the next granter."

"It didn't!"

"Or," continued Senyous evenly, "it might say that Perloo was a traitor and could not be trusted with the petal of a wilted flower."

"That's more like it."

"Oh, Great Granter," Senyous said in his raspy voice, "no doubt you have important thoughts to think. Since this—" he waved the torn proclamation —"is the smallest part of your elevated concerns— perhaps you would allow humble me to puzzle it out."

"You might as well," Berwig said in a sulky voice.

"May I say, Granter, that I appreciate that this is *your* idea. But . . . may I suggest something?"

"You can suggest anything you want," Berwig grumbled.

"Things would go better if Perloo was caught and kept from talking."

"Do you take me for a complete idiot!" Berwig bellowed.

"Oh, Granter, please," returned Senyous. "Not a complete idiot. No, not complete."

Berwig looked at Senyous with loathing.

"And my"—Senyous corrected himself—"*your* letter to the Felbarts," he asked, "have you had an answer?"

"None."

"Have no fear. There will be one. It will help a great deal." Senyous bowed, pulled his ear one more time, and turned to go but suddenly paused. "Ah! There is one other thing, Great Granter," he said.

"What's that?"

"You should send out a notice to alert the tribe as to what Perloo has done. You should be posting warriors everywhere."

"You do it," Berwig said. "My head hurts."

Senyous took two hops toward the door but paused again. "Ah, Granter, there is one other little bitsy thing."

"What's that?" Berwig said wearily.

"Where," Senyous asked, "is *my* reward?"

Berwig glared. He wanted to wring Senyous's neck. All he said, however, was, "What do you want?"

"I should like to be your first assistant, Granter. As I was to your grandfather and, for a while, to your mother. As Lucabara was to Jolaine."

"What made my mother get rid of you?"

"Lest you forget, oh, wise Granter, I resigned when she chose to become a weak leader."

"Fine. Anything you want," Berwig snapped, scratching himself. "Just do the job properly," he added even as he made up his mind to get rid of Senyous as soon as possible.

"Always pleased to oblige," Senyous whispered, and he left the room.

Once beyond Berwig's door, Senyous paused. "Good," he murmured to himself. "So far so good. Jolaine gone. Perloo almost gone. Berwig next. Then *I* shall become granter. Be sly, Senyous, be very sly."

IN THE KITCHEN

"WHICH WAY NOW?" a breathless Perloo asked Lucabara when they reached the lowest level of the burrow. Dark and dank, dripping slime, the tunnel ceilings were so low that Perloo's ears brushed against them, causing damp earth to trickle on his head.

Lucabara stood in place, tweaking her ears, sniffing with her blue nose, turning in one direction, then another.

"They'll be coming soon," Perloo reminded her, certain that Berwig or one of his warriors was going to hop out from around the next corner every moment.

"This way," Lucabara said.

It took a good while to work their way through a maze of small and large tunnels. Their variety, complexity, and age amazed Perloo. Some tunnels—the smooth ones—seemed to be well-used. Others were rough, full of rubble, poorly lit.

When Lucabara came to a large oaken door, she stopped. "This leads to the burrow kitchen," she said.

Perloo sniffed. The savory scents made his empty stomach growl.

"On the far side of the kitchen," Lucabara explained, "there's an entryway that gets you into a passage. A large chest sits there. Behind that chest is a door that leads directly outside. It hasn't been used in years, so it's not likely to be guarded. But, Perloo," she warned, "the kitchen will be full of cooks."

"It's Berwig I'm worried about," Perloo muttered, ruffling his whiskers.

"Perloo," Lucabara said with thinly veiled annoyance, "if Berwig has any brains—or if his friend Senyous has any—they will have sent out a general alarm about you."

Perloo eyed the door warily. "Maybe we should go another way."

"It's too late."

Perloo sighed. "I guess I don't have any choice but to trust you."

"Is that the best you can do?" Lucabara snapped. "Have no choice?"

"No, no! I just mean, there's no one else. Oh, dry dust . . . I didn't mean—of course I trust you. Please, I'm very upset."

Lucabara looked at him doubtfully. "The head chef is named Fergink. I know him. He was one of Jolaine's favorites. I'll do the explaining. Ready?"

When Perloo nodded Lucabara pushed open the door and the two hopped into the kitchen.

It was a long, low room, with many bays filled with

sacks, barrels, and boxes, all of which were stuffed with food. From the ceiling hung more food, yarrow, timothy, bistort, and sedge. Perloo saw goatweed, wheat, bedstraw, and ticklefoot, as well as his own favorite, scarlet falsemallow. Heaps of dried mushrooms and corn were everywhere.

Behind tables ten cooks were hard at work busily preparing food: chopping, pounding, and grinding, producing pleasing clatter and tempting aromas.

Trying to ignore his hunger, Perloo looked for the entryway that would allow them to escape. As Lucabara had said, it was on the far side of the kitchen.

"Here there, you two. What do you want?" The demand came from a squat, muscular Montmer who had been hopping about the room inspecting the work of others.

"Chef Fergink," Lucabara murmured under her breath.

The chef was a stout, middle-aged Montmer who carried himself with bulky swagger. His face was florid, with fuzzy, dust-covered, broad ears. His whiskers were unusually large, sweeping to either side of his face like the horns of a mountain goat. His thick-set legs, bare to the knees, stuck out from beneath his rabbit skin smock. But what struck Perloo most about Fergink were his arms. They bulged with muscle, no doubt from the making of preab, the roasted cake of wheat, water, and honey that was a Montmer staple.

Lucabara pulled down her left ear. Perloo hastened to do the same.

"I'm sorry to trouble you, Chef Fergink," Lucabara said, "but we were asked to bring some refreshments above."

The chef folded his massive arms over his stout chest, and looked sourly at Lucabara. "Who for?" he growled.

"Jolaine," Lucabara said.

The chef's look softened immediately. "Ah! I know you," he said. "You're Lucabara, aren't you? Granter Jolaine's first assistant."

Lucabara merely nodded.

"How's the old granter?" Fergink asked. The toughness fled from his face and voice. "Any better?"

"She's . . . she's at peace," Lucabara replied.

Glancing at her, Perloo detected a slight change of nose hue.

Fergink broke into a smile. "Anything to oblige Jolaine. By Mogwat, I worry about what's going to happen when she's gone. That Berwig . . ." He shook his head.

"Woggentip!" he called. "Get a bowl of whisk-broom parsley mixed with equal parts of chopped cheatgrass brome. And, you, Nangbur! Decant a cup of silktassel tea!"

"Hot or cold?" asked the one named Nangbur. She was young, hardly more than a cub. She looked questioningly at Lucabara.

"Warm," Lucabara said quickly.

"Of course, warm," Fergink replied, giving the order across the room. "That's the way Jolaine always takes it. Please make yourself comfortable," he said to Lucabara before continuing with the supervision of the cooks.

"That was clever," Perloo whispered.

"Just keep your ears up," Lucabara replied in an equally low voice. "And be ready to hop it if we have to."

Perloo tried to stay watchful, but found it hard while aching with hunger. At the first opportunity, when no one was looking, he grabbed a chunk of preab and bolted it down.

He was trying to figure out how he could get more when he heard Lucabara whisper, "Oh, oh! Look out!"

Two armed warriors had come through the main door. One of them had been part of the trio who had escorted Perloo from the Great Hall to the jail. The warriors hopped into the room and snapped their pikes upon the ground, making a sharp, crack-like sound.

The cooks stopped their work. Simultaneously, Lucabara and Perloo dropped behind some nearby sacks. Holding their ears down, they peeked out.

"Attention! Attention!" cried one of the warriors. "A proclamation by the new granter!" He lifted a scroll and began to read.

" 'It is hereby announced that Granter Jolaine has

been murdered in her bed! Her long, happy rule is over!' "

A cry of horror rose from the cooks. "How horrible!" "Awful!" Two cooks burst into tears and had to console one another. As for Fergink, he made a swift, furious glance in the direction of Perloo and Lucabara before returning his attention to the warriors.

The warrior continued to read from the proclamation.

" 'Berwig, Jolaine's son, following tribe laws and traditions, has swiftly and rightfully assumed the title of granter, taking on the full responsibility for running the tribe. Order will be maintained. The ceremony in which he becomes granter will take place after the normal mourning period of two weeks.'

" 'The evil one who perpetrated this ghastly deed —may his name be mud in the mouth—is Perloo. He is being vigorously hunted. It is only a matter of time before he'll be brought to judgment. Granter Berwig is offering a reward to the one who catches him. Justice will be fair, swift, and deadly!'

" 'Furthermore, because of the crisis this terrible act has precipitated, Granter Berwig, in his wisdom, has suspended all tribal freedoms and liberties. This will make the transition period simple, calm, and effective. From now on, rules, laws, regulations, judgments, and mercy will come solely from Granter Berwig.' "

This news brought shock to those in the room.

Even Lucabara and Perloo exchanged looks of surprise. "Come on, now," the warrior demanded. "Let's hear a 'Long hop Granter Berwig!' for the new granter."

There was a ragged, "Long hop Granter Berwig!"

"Let's put some feeling into it!" the second warrior shouted. "Again!" He waved his pike like a baton.

"Long hop Granter Berwig," came a louder, if not very much more enthusiastic cheer.

"That's more like it," the warrior said.

"Fergink!" cried the second warrior.

The chef, frowning, pulled down his left ear.

"Granter Berwig wants a bowl of whiskbroom parsley mixed with an equal part of chopped cheatgrass brome. And two bowls of congealed honey."

"To be sure, the parsley was Jolaine's favorite, but —" Fergink stole another glance in the direction of Lucabara and Perloo. "It's already been ordered," he replied.

Lucabara touched Perloo. "Get ready to bolt for the door we just came through," she whispered into his ear.

"Lunwel," the chef said to one of the cooks, "would you mind shutting that back door. And locking it."

"We're trapped," Perloo whispered to Lucabara.

"Woggentip," Fergink went on. "Nangbur. Did you do as you were asked before?"

The two cooks hopped forward with their bowls, looked at Fergink, stole a quick, puzzled glance where

Perloo and Lucabara had been, then turned back to the chef.

"Hop on out of here," Fergink snapped. "The new granter is waiting!"

The warriors turned smartly and hopped out, followed by Woggentip and Nangbur.

Momentarily, Fergink stood looking after them. Then he went to the front door, effectively blocking it. To his staff he said, "You've heard the terrible news about Jolaine. I want you to take some time to think and reflect. Or go search for the murderer if you prefer. Perhaps you'll get the reward. But go quickly. I want all of you out of here."

There was a scurry as the cooks hopped out of the kitchen.

As soon as they left Fergink latched the front door. Then he turned to face the place where Perloo and Lucabara had hid. "All right, you two," he cried, "come out from your hiding place."

CHEF FERGINK DECIDES

CHAPTER 12

THOUGH PERLOO KNEW they were not in the least bit guilty—other than not telling the chef the truth before—he stood before him with his head bowed.

For his part, Chef Fergink, massive arms folded over his chest, ears twitching, nose quivering, rocked back and forth on his lumpy heels.

"Lucabara," he said, growling like a bear, "I've known you a while. I thought you honest. I want the truth now."

Lucabara tipped her left ear. "There's no truth to the proclamation you just heard," she said.

"Are you saying that Granter Jolaine is alive?" Fergink demanded, flexing his arm muscles.

"That part is true. She did die."

"And did you, her most loyal assistant and friend, have anything to do with her death?" The chef's look was ferocious.

Lucabara stood flat upon her long feet and returned his gaze with steady eyes. "She died of old age and infirmities," she said.

The chef contemplated Lucabara as if he were studying an onion he wanted to peel. From time to time his eyes shifted to Perloo.

"Doesn't matter how she died," Fergink said, "Berwig is the new granter. That's bad news but it's the law."

"Fergink," Lucabara said, "she proclaimed someone else to be granter."

"Who?"

"Perloo."

"*Perloo?*" the chef exclaimed, truly surprised. "But that's the name of the murderer. The one they're looking for.".

"Nothing but cottonwood seed," Lucabara said. "Perloo is the new granter. And he's standing right before you."

Taken aback, Chef Fergink looked at Perloo with skepticism. "Are you saying *this* silly-looking, fat fellow is . . .?" He shook his head. "I need some explanation."

"Jolaine didn't trust Berwig," Lucabara began. "She thought he would become a dictator and she was right. You heard it for yourself. The first thing he did was suspend tribal freedoms."

Fergink nodded grimly. "I wasn't pleased."

"That's why Jolaine chose someone else. She wanted someone who would maintain and expand Montmer freedoms."

"Could she do that—legally?" he asked.

"Yes."

"Prove it."

Lucabara turned to Perloo.

"Well," Perloo began, "it was a long time ago—the Ram Year—the year Ertag the Early died on the field of battle during the second Montmer–Felbart War. Just before dying he chose one of his warriors to become granter. Wismark the Wise. Years later Kobolink the Generous was chosen granter because it was a time of challenge—a famine—and she was considered the cleverest of the tribe after Pilwit the Dim abdicated. Then, in the Antelope Year, there was Werluck the Wobbly who—"

"Stop!" Fergink cried. "I can't stand history. So I don't even know if what you're saying is true."

"If Perloo says so, it's true," Lucabara said. "Jolaine said he knew more of our history than anyone."

The chef shook his head. "Berwig's a lout," he said. "A swaggerer. Everybody knows that. Except they say the warriors care for him. Then there's that Senyous . . . but, look here, if Berwig is granter—"

"According to Perloo," Lucabara said, "tribal law says the granter has the right to choose."

"Is there any proof beyond what *you* say?" Fergink demanded.

Lucabara removed Jolaine's torn proclamation from her smock. "Here," she offered.

Fergink took the bark bit, studied it, then handed it back. "It makes no sense."

"Berwig ripped it," Lucabara explained. "He has

the other half. Put the pieces together and you'll see. It proclaims Perloo granter."

"*You* put it together," the chef returned sourly. "Then I'll read it."

"That's exactly what we intend to do," Lucabara said. "But first we have to get free of the burrow. Fergink, there's a way out just beyond the kitchen. Will you let us get to it?" She took a hop toward the door.

Fergink, his bulging arms crossed over his chest, stood his place and continued to stare at the two.

"You know that Berwig will make a ghastly granter," Lucabara pressed. "You said so yourself."

"And is this baggy-eyed, scruffy-whiskered, potbellied, weak-kneed fellow going to be any better?" Fergink said with a contemptuous nod toward Perloo. "Look at his legs. Dandelion stalks!"

Perloo's nose turned red.

"Jolaine thought he would do," Lucabara replied, though not with a great deal of conviction.

"And if you escape," Fergink asked Perloo, "what will you do? That is, if you really are the granter?"

Perloo, uncomfortable beneath Fergink's fierce gaze, turned to Lucabara. Her look was just as skeptical.

"Actually," Perloo mumbled, "if I am free I . . . suppose I'll try . . . I mean . . . I'll get rid of Berwig. Restore our freedoms. I guess."

"You *guess*?" Fergink said sarcastically. "How?"

Perloo appealed to Lucabara with pleading eyes. She was not about to help. Perloo ruffled his whiskers then rubbed his paws. "I'm not certain," he admitted. "But, I promise I'll try."

There was a long moment of silence. Finally Fergink said, "That's not much," he said. "But I have some preab to make. Over there," he said, gesturing toward the far end of the room. "That's all I've got to say."

With that he hopped to the far side of the room and, with his back toward Lucabara and Perloo, began to pound some grain with angry whacks of a maple stick.

"Go!" Lucabara whispered to Perloo.

The two bounded out of the kitchen and hopped down a short hall, then took an immediate left. When they reached the large chest Lucabara had mentioned, they pushed it to one side, exposing a door.

Lucabara pulled it open. This time, as she had promised, it led to the outside world. She hopped forward. Perloo hesitated. If he left the burrow, his life would change forever. If he stayed, the likelihood was that he would be killed.

"Are you afraid?" Lucabara called.

"Of course I am," Perloo replied. "I'd be a fool if I wasn't!" Saying what he felt seemed to give him just enough courage to follow Lucabara out of the burrow and into the storm.

ON RASQUICH MOUNTAIN

SNOW WAS STILL falling heavily, making it hard to see more than a few feet beyond where they stood. Drifts were higher, the air colder. The wind howled like a pack of wolves.

"Where should we go?" Perloo cried to Lucabara over the storm's din.

"That, Granter Perloo," she replied, "is your decision."

"Well then," he said, "I'm going home." He began to hop off.

For a few seconds Lucabara watched him go. Then she leaped after him, grabbed his smock and spun him around. "Perloo," she shouted into his face, "when they realize you're no longer in the Central Tribe Burrow, the first place they'll look will be your home."

"Then I don't know where to go," he cried.

Lucabara considered him with scorn. "I thought I heard you tell Chef Fergink you intended to get rid of Berwig and restore our freedoms."

"Lucabara," Perloo confessed, "I only said it to get out of there."

Lucabara reached into her smock, pulled out the split proclamation and offered it to him. "You keep this, then," she said in a voice as cold as the air.

"Lucabara," Perloo cried, "I'm no good at this sort of thing. Even if I wanted to, I don't know how to start." He felt like bursting into tears.

Gazing at him, Lucabara softened. "There's a burrow up the mountain I know about. Near the summit. Friends of mine go there during Hotair to be with snow. We can go there."

"Isn't that near Felbart territory?"

"In that general direction, yes, but don't worry, Felbarts are cowards. They would never come out in a storm like this. If they do, throw one of your snowballs at them. Your aim is good. That should be enough."

Perloo gazed uneasily into the storm. "Do you really think you can find that burrow?"

"We have to. I can't think of any other place."

The notion of hiding appealed to Perloo. Besides, Lucabara was right. His burrow would be searched. As for going to friends' burrows, he had no right to jeopardize them. "What would I do there?" he asked.

"Beside hide? You could plan a rebellion against Berwig."

"Lucabara, I hate all this!"

She snorted. "Remember what Mogwat said: 'Only the dead have no choices.'"

Perloo's nose turned red. "You sure you can find it?"

"Yes."

"At least no animals will be out and about," he thought out loud. "Fine, I'll go. But I'm not promising anything more."

"Stay close," she warned. "It's easy to get separated in a storm like this."

"Lucabara, I'm not a cub!" Perloo cried.

Lucabara spun about. "Perloo, when Jolaine told me she picked you to be granter, I had my doubts. Now that I know you, they've only increased." With that, she turned on her heels, and began to hop through the snow.

Perloo, suppressing a desire to heave a snowball at her, gave a weary sigh instead and followed.

In the best of weather Rasquich Mountain was not an easy climb. Perloo—plump and out of shape—would go twenty hops, then have to stop to catch his breath. As he paused, Lucabara moved out of sight. She did not even look back to make sure he was following. Perloo understood. She was making it clear that what he did was to be his choice, and his alone. So again and again he stumbled forward trying to catch up to the gray blob that was Lucabara.

The snow, blown in great, cutting whirls by an unceasing wind, continued to fall. The higher they went the colder it became. From time to time, though they were always moving upward, there were brief dips in the land. Then at least they could ski down. But often they slipped and fell, then struggled to right themselves.

The cold grew more intense. Piercing, biting cold; so cold Perloo thought the air itself might freeze. The snow became jagged bits of ice that wiggled like frigid worms into every nook and crevice of their smocks. His whiskers froze as sharp as needles.

Bucking directly into the bite of the storm, Perloo continued to hop upward. Ears pulled back, head down, he had no real way of knowing where he was going. He had lost track of time when, all but sleep-walking, he banged into Lucabara.

"There," she announced, "I think we're here."

Midst the swirling snow Perloo was just able to see what appeared to be a mound of snow. A smoke pipe —without smoke—stuck up.

Excited by the thought of getting out of the storm and into some warmth, they searched for the burrow door by brushing away the snow from the top of the burrow with their paws. When Lucabara finally un-covered it she scratched about for the handle, finding it quickly enough. When she pulled, however, it would not give. "Lend a paw!" she called.

The two of them pulled and pulled again. It would not give.

"Stop," Lucabara called.

"What is it?" Perloo asked.

"It must be locked," she said, turning a despairing gaze upon him. "Or frozen."

Perloo stared at her. "Then we better go back

down," he cried over the roaring wind. "We can't stay here."

"Perloo," Lucabara shouted back to make herself heard. "There's nothing safe down there. Berwig will have his warriors searching for you everywhere. It was Fergink who let up escape. Next time we won't be so lucky. We have to go on."

"Where?"

"Any place," she said wearily. "And you'll have to lead."

"Me?" Perloo cried.

"I'm exhausted," she said. "Breaking snow is hard."

Perloo looked about. The snow was like a white tornado. Winds shrieked at such a pitch his ears ached. Tall trees moaned and creaked. Every intake of air was like the swallowing of a sharp stick. "This is awful," he said through his frozen whiskers.

Without any idea of which way to go, he started off. Sometimes he took them uphill. Other times he hopped along what he thought were ridges. For all he knew they might have been hollows. It was impossible to know.

From time to time they were able to escape the wind by ducking behind some great rock—or what they believed was a rock—or squatting down in a depression. Though momentarily out of the wind, the cold remained extreme and the snow kept pouring from the sky like milk from a pot.

Even so they continued on.

The sun began to fade. The two wandering

Montmers felt an increasing numbness at the tips of their ears. Paws and toes began to tingle. It was the first sign of frostbite.

Through the frigid dusk Perloo saw what looked like a cluster of trees. Thinking that they might be somewhat better protected from the storm in such a place, he shouted, "Let's go that way!"

"Do you see something?" Lucabara called back.

"Trees! Maybe!"

She gave a nod.

They pushed on. Slow work. Excruciating work. Again and again Perloo lost sight of the trees. At times they vanished altogether. More than once Perloo felt compelled to look back over his shoulder to make sure Lucabara was following.

It was while looking back that Perloo tripped, fell, and tumbled into darkness.

A DISCOVERY

CHAPTER 14

SHRIEKING WITH FRIGHT and surprise, Perloo twisted and turned as he tumbled down. With nothing to grasp but wet, slippery snow, the more he struggled, the more he fell. The farther he fell, the darker his surroundings grew until, with a jarring thump, he came to an abrupt stop.

For a few moments he lay still, eyes closed, dazed. "Maybe I'm dead," he said out loud.

He felt himself all over. Nothing hurt. Nothing broken. He opened his eyes. He was alive but surrounded by snow. The only light—barely a glimmer —was high above. For the rest, black murk enveloped him. Though he did feel warmer, he had the good sense to know it was a delusion. He was merely out of the wind.

From a great distance he heard Lucabara. "Perloo!" she was calling. "Where are you?"

"Down here!" he shouted, all the while thrashing about to clear the snow and give himself a large breathing space.

Lucabara continued to call, her shouts growing louder and softer by turn. The next moment he heard a squawk and Lucabara came tumbling down. Stunned, she lay a short way off.

Perloo struggled to her side. "Are you all right?"

"I think so," she said weakly. "Where are we?"

"Down some snow hole or crevice."

"The proclamation!" Lucabara cried and dove into her smock. "It's all right," she said with relief.

She looked out. "Perloo," she said. "If we don't get out of here we'll soon freeze to death."

Pushing and digging, they worked to enlarge the area into which they had fallen. As they struggled Perloo struck hardness. "There seems to be some kind of wall here," he announced.

Lucabara felt about with her paws. "Rock face," she announced. "We can't dig through that. But rock is never completely smooth. There may be some cracks, some gaps—maybe even a cave—something into which we could squeeze. Our smocks might keep us alive till morning."

Working in what had become total darkness, Perloo felt about. The more he worked the more he sensed that they had fallen into a gorge, perhaps a narrow canyon.

It was while groping over the rock surface that Perloo touched something round, hard, and smooth. Feeling about carefully he decided it was a wooden ring affixed to the wall. "Lucabara," he called. "I've found something."

Lucabara pawed the ring. "A grip," she said excitedly. "Maybe it's attached to a door."

Perloo hesitated. "Lucabara," he warned, "Montmers don't use rings on doors."

"Well, we can't stay here," Lucabara replied and gave the ring a jerk. Nothing happened. "Come on," she urged, "give a paw."

The two pulled as hard as they could. This time there was some movement.

"Again!" Lucabara urged.

With a sharp crack—the sound of ice breaking—a door opened a bit. Beyond, they could see faint, glimmering light. Perloo and Lucabara exchanged looks. If there was light, someone—or thing—had to be inside.

"Pull again," Lucabara said, but more softly than before. The door creaked open.

Lucabara squeezed inside first. Perloo followed. With care they shut the door behind them, but not so tightly that if the need came it would be hard to reopen quickly.

Exhausted, Perloo and Lucabara squatted down, took deep breaths, and rubbed their toes and ears. Only then did they look about. They were in an immense cave, dry and warm with a floor of hardpacked earth. Walls were rough, black volcanic rock. From the ceiling hung stalactites that looked like jagged, gleaming teeth.

"Do you think something lives here?" Lucabara asked, feeling the need to keep her voice low.

"Bears, perhaps. Mountain lions. Or Felbarts. They live in caves."

A startled look came to Lucabara's eyes. "I don't know much about Felbarts," she said, "except that they're hateful, cowardly creatures."

"We have fought them in many wars," Perloo agreed. He wished he could see better. The cave was too gloomy.

"In all your reading," Lucabara asked, "did you ever discover what makes them hate us so?"

"It's land we feud about. Borders. Who can live where. To tell the truth, sometimes it's we Montmers who are greedy."

"I doubt that," Lucabara said.

"It's what I read," Perloo returned.

Lucabara stood up. "Come on," she said. "We better see where the cave leads."

Reluctant as ever, Perloo tagged along, hopping forward silently. His ears—no longer numb from the storm—were quivering, trying to make some sense of the curious sounds he was beginning to detect. He also smelled something strange. "There's something bad," he whispered.

"I know," she acknowledged.

Perloo pointed into a corner of the cave. "Look!" There lay a pile of old, white bones.

"Meat eaters," Lucabara said with a barely suppressed shudder.

They continued on, but more cautiously. The farther they went, the more distinct were the sounds and smells. At first Perloo could not make sense of it. Then it occurred to him that the noise was like a heartbeat, as if some great beast was before them.

He checked over his shoulder to make certain the way back was unobstructed. Just in case . . .

They reached a pile of boulders jumbled together. Through the gaps of the tumbled mass, they could see a large open area. In the middle logs were burning. On racks over the fire great chunks of meat were being roasted. Scattered bones lay strewn about the ground. The air was smoky.

Twenty short, lean creatures with coyote-like heads, hairy, human-like bodies, and bushy tails that continually twitched, were sitting about the fire. Their panting mouths revealed lolling tongues and fangs that glistened by the light of the fire. In their five-fingered clawed hands were clubs made from heavy bones. They were Felbarts.

The Felbarts were wearing wooden, bowl-shaped helmets in which holes had been cut to accommodate their short, pointy ears. Their bodies were covered by leather jerkins over which wooden bibs—armor— had been fitted.

At the head of the group sat a particularly elderly Felbart. The leather jerkin that covered his body was decorated with porcupine quills and small, multicolored stones. He alone wore no helmet.

Small in stature, his long, thin, coyote face had a sharp, runny black nose, large dark eyes, and pointy eyes. His scanty whiskers were gray. Though fur-covered, the left side of his face revealed a scar. His tail—what Perloo could see of it—was ragged. His hands and feet were gnarled. He was missing teeth. Before him was a drum that he was beating steadily with a bone club. After playing for a while, he lifted his snout and began a yelping chant:

At the time of Coldwinds when icy winds wither all,
When the only colors are hues of white,
When the earth becomes as hard as stone,
Our hearts are better prepared for long marches
And hard battles.
We ready ourselves for the struggle
Against our cruel Montmer enemies who seek
To take our lands from us.
But our Felbart hearts are strong and ready,
Ready to fight for Felbart Freedoms!

As the old Felbart continued to beat his drum the other Felbarts barked his words. Now one, now another, arched a head back and broke into a deep-throated frenzy of yip-yapping and long, drawn out howling that reverberated through the cave.

Perloo, heart hammering, could hardly breathe from fright. Wanting to get Lucabara's attention, he turned toward her. It was then that he saw seven Felbart warriors—armed with bone clubs—creeping stealthily in their direction.

THE FELBARTS

CHAPTER 15

"LUCABARA!" PERLOO CRIED. "Behind us!"

Lucabara spun about, saw the Felbarts, and instantly dove between two of them, managing to avoid their grasping hands and snarling jaws. Once free she went bounding off.

The Felbarts, caught off guard, fell over themselves in confusion. In the barking, yelping uproar, Perloo eluded them too. He began to hop madly after his friend. Upon reaching a bend, they took it, only to discover they had run into a rock-faced, dead end. They whirled. It was too late. The Felbarts were upon them.

"Fight for your life!" Lucabara shouted as she squared her feet into a fighting stance.

Perloo tried to get ready, but his legs were shaking so much, he could not.

Barking furiously, lips drawn back to reveal fangs, the Felbarts advanced with bone clubs held aloft, ready to strike. "Surrender or your life!" one of them cried.

Lucabara prepared herself to kick. Before she

could, Perloo yanked down both ears, the Montmer sign of surrender. "I give up! I give up!" he screamed.

"Perloo," Lucabara cried. "Fight!"

Instead Perloo made a small hop forward, delivering himself into Felbart paws. Working deftly, they flung grass ropes about his ankles to keep him from hopping off again. The next thing Perloo heard was Lucabara calling, "I give up too."

Prodded by growls and bared teeth, as well as jabs of bone clubs, the Felbarts herded the Montmers back to the place from which they had fled.

As Perloo and Lucabara approached the pack, all Felbart eyes—full of anger—were on them. Teeth gnashed. Tails twitched.

The old Felbart, who had been playing the drum, rose up. The fur along his back and tail stood on end. His ears lay flat. From within his throat came a deep-throated growl.

"You are Montmers," the old Felbart barked. Though a statement of fact, it was delivered like an accusation.

Not knowing what else to do—and wanting to show he meant no harm—Perloo reached up and pulled his left ear down. "Well, yes, that's true," he admitted. "And may the sun rise clear over your mountain."

The old Felbart grunted disparagingly. "Who are you?" he demanded. "What are you doing here?"

Perloo stole a glance at Lucabara. She was staring before her with stubborn pride. Perloo was not so sure that was a good response. After all, it was they who had intruded into Felbart territory.

"My name is Perloo," he replied. "This is my friend Lucabara. We lost our way in the storm, fell through the snow and then came upon the entryway to your cave."

"It's not just a storm," the old Felbart said. "It's one of the worst blizzards in years. Montmers rarely come here in the best of seasons. You're too cowardly. Why were you wandering about during such conditions?"

"Please, may I have the honor of sharing your name?" Perloo requested.

The old Felbart cocked his head. His ears flicked. "My name is Weyanto," he said in haughty tones. "*Packmaster* Weyanto."

Perloo and Lucabara gave a start. Just as Montmers used the term *granter* for the head of their tribe, the Felbarts used *packmaster* for their leader. The meaning was perfectly clear. They had stumbled into the den of the chief Felbart.

Perloo's nose turned purple. He quickly pulled his ear again. "I had . . . no idea," he sputtered.

"For a Montmer to come into our cave," Weyanto snapped, "at this time, in the fashion you have done—secretly—without requesting permission, to be discovered spying upon us, these are all provocative acts. Have you any idea how we treat spies, in particular Montmer spies?"

Perloo shook his head.

"We use our jaws to snap their necks."

Perloo felt faint.

"Did Granter Jolaine, your cunning leader, send you here to spy on us?" asked Weyanto.

"I . . . assure you, Packmaster," Perloo stammered, "we weren't spying. We really did lose our way and tumbled through the snow to your den entrance. As for Granter Jolaine—well, just yesterday . . . she died."

"Jolaine *dead*?" Weyanto cried. There was a gasp from the other Felbarts, followed by intense murmuring. A few began to bark. One Felbart lifted her head and howled so mournfully, the cave reverberated with her cry.

Perloo and Lucabara hardly knew what to make of the hullabaloo.

The packmaster stared at Perloo with new ferocity. "I suppose," he said, "it's that pup of hers, Berwig, who has become the new granter."

The question instantly stilled the other Felbarts. They looked at Perloo and waited for his answer.

Worrying his paws, Perloo stole another glance at Lucabara. Instead of returning his look she said, "So Berwig claims."

The old Felbart turned on her savagely. "Merely *claims*? What does *that* mean?" he barked.

Lucabara looked at him coolly. "He's in control of our Central Tribe Burrow," was her answer.

The packmaster gazed at her, head cocked to one side. "Does Jolaine's death," he asked, "have anything to do with your being lost?"

When Lucabara said nothing, Weyanto turned back

to Perloo. Perloo was still uncertain what to say. Though clearly the news of Jolaine's death had distressed the Felbarts greatly, and even made things worse, he had no idea why.

"I asked you a question," Weyanto pressed.

Perloo, fearful of what the Felbarts might do if they learned he was granter, said, "Packmaster, may I speak to you privately?"

Weyanto studied Perloo's face intently. His ears lifted. "Why should I?" he demanded.

"There's something I need to explain," Perloo offered. "But I don't think this is the best place to talk. I won't try to escape again. I promise."

After a moment's further reflection, during which he scratched hard under his chin with his claw-tipped fingers, the packmaster nodded to one of the Felbarts. This Felbart unbound Perloo's legs. Weyanto called out the name of another and told her to follow closely but to kill Perloo if he attempted to escape. Then he began to walk away.

Perloo hopped after him. Suddenly Lucabara called, "Perloo, don't forget. They're our enemies!"

Perloo ducked his head but continued on.

As he followed Weyanto, Perloo had a chance to observe the cave. It was very large, with corridors leading off in many directions. Any number of Felbarts, from positions of safety, were staring at him with intense, malevolent glares.

Perloo did notice many paintings on the walls, fine renditions of the wars between the Montmers and

Felbarts. Everything was depicted from a Felbart point of view. To his amazement he saw images of Mogwat in them. What's more, she was always on the Felbart side.

Weyanto bid Perloo enter a small room that had been hewn from the rock. The rough stone walls were bare of ornamentation. There were no furnishings. The air was cold, damp. Partially gnawed bones lay everywhere. The smell of rancid meat made Perloo feel ill.

After telling the guard to remain near the entryway, Weyanto sat on the floor, his tail—behind him—twitching. Perloo squatted.

The two appraised one another in silence. It was the old Felbart who began to speak. "Our great teacher, Mogwat, once said, 'If you learn to know your enemy before you hate him, you may learn not to have an enemy.' "

"How do you know about Mogwat?" Perloo asked.

"Why shouldn't we know?" returned Weyanto angrily.

"I just didn't think you would, that's all," Perloo murmured.

"You Montmers think Felbarts are ignorant beasts, don't you? Let me assure you, Montmer, we Felbarts have our laws, culture, and history. We have families and pups. We have art. We have stories. We have our cowards, but we have many more heroes."

An abashed Perloo said, "Forgive me, Packmaster. I didn't mean to suggest anything bad about Felbarts. It's just that, well, as Mogwat said, 'To see the world with the eyes of others is to stand atop a new mountain.' "

The packmaster gave a growl of appreciation. "You know Mogwat."

"She is our great teacher too," Perloo offered.

"Then you are wiser than I thought," returned the packmaster, making a slight curl of his upper lip that Perloo interpreted as a hint of a smile. "You give me some hope. But again, I must ask you, why have you come here?"

"My friend and I were lost in the storm."

"That's the easy truth," the packmaster returned. "You know as well as I do, the real question is, *why* were you wandering? I suspect it has something to do with—if what you say is true—the death of Granter Jolaine."

As quickly as he could Perloo told Weyanto all that had happened from the moment Lucabara summoned him, to their escape from the Central Tribe Burrow.

When he was done Weyanto studied Perloo so intently the Montmer felt he was being measured. At last the packmaster said, "Then it is your belief, Perloo, that you are the new Montmer granter."

"I think so."

"And it was nothing you expected?"

"Oh, no. Not at all."

"Are you pleased with your new position?"

"I wish . . . I wish Jolaine had chosen someone else."

Weyanto's face softened. He licked his nose, then nodded. "It is as Mogwat said, 'You are never more alone than when you are followed by many.' Regardless, will you accept the title?"

Perloo shrugged. "I don't want to, but . . ."

"Perloo, have you any proof of your story, other than your words?" the packmaster asked.

"Not really. Lucabara has only half of Jolaine's proclamation."

"And the other half?"

"Berwig has it."

Weyanto closed his large eyes to think out a decision, during which he scratched himself vigorously behind an ear. At last he opened his eyes. "Before I tell you whether or not I believe you," he began, "there is something you must know first. No doubt you observed that we are preparing for war."

"I did."

"Do you know why? Or against whom?"

"No."

"Well, then, Granter Perloo, if that's who you are, please know," said Weyanto as he pointed a finger right at Perloo, "that we are preparing for war against you."

WAR

CHAPTER 16

"WAR AGAINST ME?" Perloo cried. "What are you talking about?"

"Surely among Montmers there is talk, gossip, rumor."

"Oh, bird's teeth," Perloo said. "If you asked me I could tell you anything you wanted to know about the politics of Fiklow the Proud, or even Eldor the Empty, but I don't know much about politics *now.*"

"Perloo," Weyanto said, "didn't Mogwat tell us that 'Ignorance is the cruelest weather.' "

Perloo said nothing.

"Your tale," Weyanto continued, "is difficult to believe: Hauled out of your burrow, proclaimed as granter, you insist you know nothing about what is happening."

"It's true!" Perloo insisted.

The packmaster reached into his jerkin and pulled out a sheet of bark. "This was sent to me. It came from Berwig. Read it," Weyanto said somberly.

Perloo took the letter into his paws:

To: Packmaster Weyanto of the Felbart Tribe
From: Berwig the Big, Heir to the title of
       Montmer Granter

Be advised! My esteemed mother, Jolaine the
Good, is in poor health. She is not expected to
live long. When she dies it is I who—as a matter
of course—shall become Granter. When the time
comes to take my place on the Settop it will be
my duty to take up the dragonfly wing pike, and
lead my Montmer warriors into all those lands
and territories east of Tingwort Creek that rightfully belong to the Montmer tribe.

When you hear of Jolaine's death, be warned!
You are hearing a declaration of war!

In this I have the support of all Montmers. Indeed, many have begged that I take this action.

I therefore urge you to accept our claims, and
retreat as soon as possible from your illegally
held lands, and so save the spilling of Felbart
blood.

Signed,
Berwig the Big, Granter to be!

"Oh, dry dust," Perloo murmured. "When did this come?"

"Some twenty moon-glows ago."

"Where is Tingwort Creek?"

"It's not on any map we know."

"Have you expanded your territory?"

"No."

"Then nothing is true here," Perloo cried, "except that Jolaine was dying."

"Perloo," Weyanto snapped with bitterness, "you just claimed you knew nothing of what passes for politics in your tribe these days. How can you now be so sure this letter isn't speaking the truth?"

"Packmaster," Perloo protested, "I had many talks with Jolaine. She never talked—even hinted—about making war against you Felbarts. In my last conversation with her, she warned that Berwig might be contemplating war against you. It was one of her reasons for not making him granter."

"If Jolaine is dead," Weyanto said, "who is granter?"

"I . . . suppose I am."

"But didn't you inform me you did not want to be granter?"

"Well, yes . . ."

"Then who am I to deal with?" Weyanto yelped. "You or Berwig?"

Perloo rubbed his paws. "I suppose . . . me."

"Have you *any* followers back there? Any who honor you as granter, who will come to your side?"

Perloo thought for a moment. "There's my friend, Lucabara," he said.

"Just her?"

"There was a chef, Fergink. But I'm not so sure about him."

"Then there isn't much you can do, is there?" the Felbart snapped. "Berwig is in control. What if he *is* planning to invade us?

"Montmer," the packmaster went on, "if I'm to believe you, you'll need to find a way to prove what you say. For all I know you're part of an elaborate trick to lull us. Perhaps even as we speak—under cover of this storm—Berwig is assembling Montmer warriors and hopping in our direction."

"Even if he was," Perloo offered, "I don't think his army could move now. There is the blizzard. So we have some time."

The packmaster gazed at Perloo.

"I will think about it," Weyanto said. "You must too. You are right. We have a little time. In the meanwhile . . ." Weyanto lifted his snout. "Put this Montmer in the big cell," he barked to the guard. "Treat him well, but make sure he doesn't escape."

Perloo didn't know if it was deliberate on Weyanto's part, but the path upon which he was led took him along the edge of a large open area in the cave. There, by the light of burning torches, he observed packs of Felbarts in ranks and rows. All were helmeted and bibbed. All were marching in military order, uttering ferocious war barks as they went through elaborate military drills.

The stone cell in which Perloo was placed was bare but perfectly clean. It contained a lit candle as well as a fresh pile of straw. On the wall hung an image of Mogwat.

Perloo studied it intensely. When he compared it to the Montmer images of the bird, there were some differences: perhaps the Felbarts made the blue of her feathers darker, her eyes wider. But still, without doubt, it was Mogwat.

Perloo tried to recall the origins of the story of Mogwat, how she came to be the sage of the Montmers.

He knew that the book, *The Adventures of Mogwat the Magpie*, was from a time when mountain animals were at constant war upon one another. Though birds lived their own lives, Mogwat, a magpie, after many extraordinary adventures, brought peace to the mountain. Later, her life and sayings were collected. Still, it had never occurred to Perloo that others who lived on the mountains venerated her too. The notion fascinated and pleased him at the same time. It also reminded him of one of Mogwat's sayings, "Truth is often painful to speak but soothing to live."

In the room, next to a jar of water, was a plate of something round, presumably eatable. Feeling starved, Perloo picked one up and sniffed at it. To his relief it didn't smell like meat. He took a careful nibble. To his surprise, though it had a slightly different taste and was round, it was very much like preab. The differences were not enough to deter Perloo. He devoured the bowl's contents.

After eating, Perloo squatted against a wall and began to ponder what had happened to him. After all, it was but a short time ago that he had been in bed in his snug burrow, utterly content with reading and sleeping the Coldcross away. Since then, there had been so much hopping about, so much fleeing, falling, in and out of cells. . . .

He wondered where the Felbarts had taken Lucabara, if she were in some kind of danger. Though he worried about her, missed her, he realized there was nothing he could do but be patient. If he had been in his own snug burrow, he'd probably be sipping tea and reading about an ancient war—and enjoying it. Now he was in a cave and trying to figure out how to stop a real war. Like it or not, his life had changed.

THE LABORS OF SENYOUS

ALL THAT NIGHT the great blizzard roared over Rasquich Mountain. Winds blew. Snow fell. The temperature dropped and dropped again until the air seemed to congeal into implacable ice. Not a living creature was abroad. All were hiding in burrows, nests, or dens near whatever heat they could find, be it fire, fur, or friend. The one exception was Senyous, Senyous the Sly.

Deep within the Montmer Central Tribe Burrow, in a small, sparse room where a single candle gleamed, Senyous squatted, wide awake. Half of Jolaine's proclamation lay before him. Nose quivering, ears trembling, he read it again and again and again.

From time to time, he would hop up, grasp the sharp pike that leaned against the wall, and go through a violent exercise of thrust, parry, deflect, and attack. Though Senyous was small, though he limped, though he was decrepit in appearance, the old Montmer took great delight in his skill with a pike. Not only was it the one thing he did to relax, it helped him think. Even so, he was careful to keep his prowess private, using it only when needed. As for those who did discover his talent, they did not live long enough to tell others about it. So the secret remained.

After much thought—and pike work—Senyous took up one of his writing sticks, held its point in the candle flame, and charred it to a sooty blackness. Then he wrote Jolaine's words—incomplete as they were—on a scrap of bark. Pondering long and hard, he began to write new words.

It took Senyous the rest of the night, with deep thought and much rewriting, to get the proclamation to read as he desired. Then he studied the paw writing style on the original piece and practiced imitating that until he could copy Jolaine's style with exactitude.

All that accomplished, he searched out and found a piece of bark that was close to the look and feel of Jolaine's original proclamation. Once he found it he tore the new piece so it fitted the original perfectly. Finally, he glued the two pieces together so that it was almost impossible to see the seam.

Now Senyous wrote out his words on the new piece of bark in the exact style of the original writing. When done, the proclamation read:

I, Jolaine, the sixty-third Granter
But not being the First have
Come to the end of life.

Since I wish the Montmer
Tribe to be free in the pursuit of
truth,

I wish to state that Perloo appears bent
Upon doing ill to all Montmers and seeks to
Take all power unto himself:

Since I, Jolaine, as Granter have the right,
When defending freedom, to proclaim anyone in the Tribe
A traitor,

So I proclaim my former friend Perloo to be
An outlaw, deprived of all rights and privileges of
This tribe. I have the hope and expectation that he
Will be punished and denied the freedom of every
Kind.

JOLAINE

Senyous read and reread the document with intense gratification, occasionally grunting with glee. What pleased him most—aside from what the text now said about Perloo—was that it made no mention of Berwig.

It was dawn when Senyous reached Berwig's rooms and tapped upon the door.

"Who is it?" growled a sleeping Berwig.

"It's me, Senyous."

"Go away! I need my sleep."

Senyous gritted his teeth. "Exulted Granter," he pleaded, "may I have a brief moment of your active life? I've done a little work that should bring you joy. Even for one whose life is crowded with momentous events such as yours, it's important."

"Oh, all right," returned Berwig in a sulky voice. "Come in."

Senyous hopped quietly into the room.

Berwig was sprawled upon his bed surrounded by partially eaten pots of food.

"Make it quick," Berwig murmured as he stuffed his mouth with wilted parsley and prickly pear mash.

"Granter Berwig," Senyous said, "I humbly beg to show you a trifle." He held out the reconstructed document.

Frowning, and with a show of indifference, Berwig took up the bark sheet. He squinted at it, shifted a wilted candle so as to see better, studied it anew. As he read he kept darting sidelong glances at Senyous. Berwig was sure he was after something.

Berwig liked what he read. He wished he'd done it. Not that he had any intention of giving Senyous the satisfaction of knowing *that*. Instead, he made a point of glowering, rubbing his eyes, scratching himself, stuffing more foul food into his mouth, then tossing the sheet away so that it landed midst food scraps.

It took all of Senyous's willpower to keep himself from leaping forward and snatching it up.

"Well," Berwig grunted, "what about it?"

Senyous forced his thin lips into a smile. "Are you pleased with my work, oh, glorious Granter?"

"It's all right," Berwig allowed. "I suppose you want some reward."

"Your trust is my reward," Senyous said with another deep bow.

"Good," Berwig smirked. "That's all you're going to get."

"Begging your pardon, Granter," said Senyous. "But what are you going to *do* with this proclamation?"

"I haven't made up my mind."

"If I may be so bold, Granter, I believe it should be read then posted in the Great Hall so all may see it. The tribe—in its folly—trusted Jolaine," Senyous explained. "The fact that I've . . . *adjusted* her own words will be of immense value in our dealings with Perloo. May I have your permission to read it quickly and then post it?"

"That's for me to do," returned Berwig, fearful of letting anyone other than he become the center of attention. "You're to keep as far in the background as possible. You're not liked, Senyous. Not the way I am."

"It is my honor to agree," Senyous said with a pull at his left ear. "But today, right after early feed you should read it."

"Fine, fine . . ."

Senyous had one paw on the doorway when he paused. "Has there been any word about . . . Perloo?"

"Oh, yes," Berwig replied, effecting nonchalance. "He escaped." His nose turned purple.

Senyous spun around. "*Escaped!* How?"

"It was the kitchen chef. Fergink. He let them get out. Don't worry. I threw him in jail."

"But . . . but," Senyous stammered, "Perloo at large is dangerous! He'll bring about a rebellion."

Berwig had been furious and alarmed when he had learned about Perloo's escape. Now, before Senyous, he simply scratched himself. "Oh, calm yourself. He's nothing. I'm granter. He can't do me any harm now."

"Of course he can!" Senyous bleated. "You know perfectly well Jolaine intended *him* to be granter. Don't be a fool, Berwig!"

"Don't call me a fool!" Berwig bellowed, spewing and spraying crumbs as he yelled. "I'm granter! Anyway, he went into the blizzard. Probably froze to death."

"Have you checked his burrow?" Senyous asked.

Berwig, who had done absolutely nothing about Perloo, said, "If you're so nervous about him, you do something."

"Was Lucabara with him?"

"Yes."

"May I suggest you announce they've joined up with the Felbarts."

Alarmed, Berwig sat up. "The Felbarts! Is that true?"

"How do I know!" Senyous returned, glaring at Berwig angrily. "Are you trying to find out what's true or are you trying to stay in power?"

"Stay in power, of course."

"Good. I will need warriors to send out patrols," Senyous said. "We must suppress all opposition before it starts. Beyond that, it's time we acted on the matter of those Felbarts."

Berwig squinted at Senyous. "You have no respect for me, do you?"

"Respect," Senyous said with contempt. "Do you think you can keep the Settop out of *respect*?" he demanded. "Berwig, we must have that war. Saying that Perloo has joined the Felbarts will help. It will pressure the tribe into submission."

"Go away!"

"With your kind permission," he sneered, "I will." So saying, he hopped out of the room, slamming the door behind him.

BERWIG, SENYOUS, AND . . . GUMPEL

LEFT ALONE, BERWIG scratched himself all over, giving particular care to behind his ears and under his chin. "I detest Senyous," he grumbled to himself. "He treats me with nothing but disdain. But, by Mogwat, *I'm* the granter! Not him! Very well, I'll *make* him understand." He reached for the bellpull and jangled it. Within moments there was a tap on the door.

"Enter!"

A warrior hopped into the room and pulled his left ear, then waited for orders.

"Find Gumpel. Tell her I need her."

"Yes, Granter." The warrior withdrew, and Berwig, still muttering oaths against Senyous, began to eat while waiting impatiently.

Upon leaving Berwig, Senyous had hovered about the granter's door wondering if anything would happen. He did not have too long to wait. The warrior Berwig summoned arrived, met with the granter, then left.

"Stop!" Senyous called as soon as the warrior emerged from Berwig's room.

The warrior halted.

"Do you know me?" Senyous demanded.

"Senyous. First assistant to the granter."

"Right! Pull your ear!"

The warrior did so.

"It's my job," Senyous said, "to make sure everything the granter requests is done properly and quickly. Do you understand?"

The warrior nodded.

"He sent for you and, I presume, gave you an order. What was it?"

"To fetch Gumpel."

"Gumpel!" Senyous exclaimed in surprise. "Well then, do it quickly, but after she meets with Berwig you are to bring her directly to me. Do you understand? *Me*. Immediately!"

The warrior pulled at his ear and hurried off.

"Gumpel," muttered Senyous angrily as he hopped away. "Detestable creature."

Not long after, Berwig, sitting in his room eating, heard a tap on his door.

"Share your name!"

"Gumpel, oh, Granter," came a soft whisper.

"Enter!"

The door opened very slowly. At first Berwig thought no one was there. Then Gumpel put her head around the door. She was a short, squat, round Montmer, with bleary eyes and floppy ears. Her mouth was slack. Her feet smelled like old pigeon nests and her smock of mole fur was grimy. When she moved—which she did as infrequently as possible—it was like a wet slug.

Solitary by nature, she avoided all, even as she was avoided by all. But by being thoroughly ignored, she was able to move through the tribe as if invisible. Though Berwig had employed Gumpel any number of times as his personal spy, he looked upon her with disgust.

"Did you send for me?" Gumpel said. Her voice was soft, and she uttered sentences with irritating pauses between each word.

"Yes."

Gumpel oozed into the room like a spreading stain.

Berwig, midst his own slop and filth, felt the need to wave a paw before his nose to dispel her smell. "I suppose," he said, "you know Senyous."

Gumpel lifted a shoulder and let it drop. "I think so."

"Spy on him. Report to me about what he does, who he meets with, and whatever gossip you might muck up."

"As you wish, Granter," Gumpel said sleepily, and slipped out of the room as noiselessly as she had come.

The moment Gumpel hopped from the room, the warrior approached her. "Senyous desires to see you," he said.

Gumpel paused, peered up at the warrior with

lidded eyes, then glanced toward Berwig's room. "As you wish," she mumbled.

Senyous and Gumpel met at the very bottom of the Central Tribe Burrow in a small, dingy room. Senyous's eyes were alert, attentive. Gumpel's eyes suggested she was about to fall down from exhaustion.

Senyous smiled thinly. "I have always admired you," he said in his feathery voice.

Gumpel looked up—as if surprised to hear anyone speak. "Have you?" she muttered. "How very generous."

"Quiet, careful, loyal work is what I admire," Senyous said, toying with his tattered smock so as to bring attention to its decrepitude.

"And I, Senyous, I like modesty and . . . humility." The old Montmer snorted slyly. "Ah! We know each other well."

"Perhaps," Gumpel said with a yawn while taking note of Senyous's sharp pike that lay on the ground close to his paw.

"All the more reason, then," Senyous said, "not to waste time. I believe you are working for Berwig."

"I never know," Gumpel replied, "who I work for. Sometimes I work for this one. Sometimes another." She yawned so widely Senyous was forced to observe her tonsils. "I've been known to lose my way," she said slowly.

"And how, Gumpel, do you solve *that* problem?"

"By always speaking the truth."

"Very well then," pressed Senyous. "I believe Berwig sent you to spy on me. Is *that* true?"

Gumpel pulled down an ear, gazed at its tip, then began to pick upon some matted hairballs on her arm. "Why," she drawled, "should you even think such a thing?"

"Because," Senyous hissed, "it is my *nature* to think such things. Come, come, Gumpel," he said, unable to suppress his impatience, "we both know what we're about."

Gumpel sighed. "I suppose."

Senyous—trying to pay no mind to Gumpel's smell—leaned forward. "Gumpel," he whispered, "have you considered that it might save time and energy if we worked—*together?*"

"I'm always in favor of saving energy," Gumpel replied listlessly.

"What," Senyous asked, "do you think of Berwig?"

"Senyous," she said, "thinking may be all right for some, but for me, thinking is . . . exhausting."

Senyous inched closer. Their noses—his dry, cracked, and gray, hers sticky, moist, and pale green—almost touched. "Gumpel," he whispered, struggling to keep from gagging, "I believe a war is coming."

Gumpel's bleary eyes widened a fraction. "Is there?" she said. "Between whom?"

"The Montmers against the Felbarts."

"Is this . . . good?" she asked.

"It will be good for you and me," Senyous

informed her. "Berwig will hop off at the head of the army, and . . ." His voice trailed off.

"And *what?*" Gumpel asked, blinking with the effort of asking still another question.

"Many will be hurt or even killed."

"Are you talking about Berwig?" murmured Gumpel.

"Perhaps."

"That would be . . . awful," Gumpel said. "Who would be granter then?"

"To speak the truth," Senyous confided, "I have never given the question much thought. But, since you ask, who would be the granter? Well, perhaps— you."

"*Me?*" Gumpel exclaimed.

"Why not?" Senyous suggested. "It can be *anyone.*"

Gumpel stared at Senyous. There was nothing sleepy about her now. She sat erect. Her stumpy ears stood tall. Her mouth went slack. Her nose dripped with excitement. Her eyes watered. The next moment, however, she collapsed upon herself like a decaying puffball. "No, not me," she said, wiping her nose with an ear. "Too strenuous.

"But, you, Senyous, you would make a fine granter. And your . . . loyalty is well known."

Senyous nodded. "Especially," he said, "to those who help *me.*"

"As you wish," Gumpel mumbled, and the two gazed at one another. "I must go," she said, heaving

herself up. "Berwig wished me to report about you."
So saying, she slunk away.

As she went, Senyous reached for his pike and
hefted it. Why not, he thought, kill the harpy now and
be done with her? Deceitful, treacherous creature!

Instead, he put the pike aside and with a burst of
energy, hopped down a tunnel until he came to a
small room that contained a ladder. The ladder went
straight up until it came to a ledge just outside
Berwig's private chambers. As soon as Senyous got
there he squatted down, content to wait and listen.

Gumpel, meanwhile, made her slow way back to
Berwig's quarters. She was trying to decide what to
say to him. "Tell the truth," she decided. "Some of it,
anyway."

Halfway to Berwig's room she halted. "But I do
believe," she mumbled, "Senyous was right. I would be
a good granter. A sweet, lovely granter."

Within moments Gumpel was standing before
Berwig. He was reclining on his bed, eating and
scratching.

"Well," he demanded, "what's Senyous up to?"

"War with the Felbarts."

Berwig dismissed the notion with a wave of his
sticky paw. "I know about that," he snapped. "He
thinks the tribe will support me if there's a war."

"Granter," Gumpel said, "Senyous does not want
you to lead the army against the Felbarts."

"Why not?"

"He thinks you'll get too much glory. Become too

powerful. He fears you will be such a fine warrior no-body will notice him."

"Did he really say that?" Berwig asked.

"Do you think I would lie?" Gumpel replied.

"Sly, vicious Senyous," Berwig snarled. "Go away," he barked. "I have to plan this war of mine."

"Will the war happen?" Gumpel asked.

"That's my business!" Berwig snapped.

"As you wish," Gumpel murmured as she oozed out of the room.

"By Mogwat," Berwig said out loud to himself while working on an itch that had settled into the small of his back. "I *will* have this war. What's more, I'll go at the head of the army! That'll show Senyous!" So saying he stretched for a bowl of honey and a plate of preab and began to gorge himself.

Senyous, having heard Gumpel and Berwig's entire conversation as well as Berwig's private rumblings, fairly purred with satisfaction as he heeled down the ladder.

PERLOO AND LUCABARA PLAN

WHEN PERLOO WOKE from a restless sleep he discovered that visitors had come. There were new candles. The preab bowl had been renewed. And on the other side of the room lay . . . Lucabara!

Eager to talk to her, he hopped up, but when he realized she was asleep he made himself sit quietly, munching on the quaint-tasting preab.

While waiting for his companion to wake, Perloo attempted to sort out what he'd learned from his talk with Weyanto. Berwig's letter made it perfectly clear that he was intent upon leading the Montmers into a war against the Felbarts. The question was, why?

Rummaging through his knowledge of history, the best Perloo could come up with were the events pertaining to Granter Wentlow. While it was true that most Montmer–Felbart wars seemed to be about territory, Perloo recalled that Granter Wentlow the Winless, when most unpopular, declared war upon the Felbarts in hopes that Montmers would rally around him. His military adventures fared just as miserably as did his home rule. Happily—for the good of the tribe—he took ill and died peacefully in his smock.

"Oh, dry dust," Perloo mused. "I suppose Berwig's attempting the same thing: trying to force the tribe into supporting him."

Shortly after, Lucabara woke. "What happened when you went off with the packmaster?" she asked.

"I told him everything."

"Perloo, they're our enemies!"

"I'm not so sure," he said and gave her an account of his talk with the packmaster, including Berwig's virtual declaration of war.

"There," he said, when done, "do you still think it was wrong to tell Weyanto who I was and why we had come?"

"We'll have to see," Lucabara allowed grudgingly.

"Lucabara, you live in the Central Tribe Burrow; did you hear anything about wanting a war against the Felbarts?"

"Nothing," she said.

Perloo told her about Granter Wentlow. "I think that's what this war is about," he said. "Just a way to get the tribe to support Berwig."

"If it is, it's Senyous's doing. You do know," she said, "that he once was Jolaine's first assistant?"

"He was? What happened?"

"It was when Jolaine decided we needed more freedoms," Lucabara explained. "Senyous told her she was a weak granter, and that, being widowed, if she coupled with him and let him take over, all would be restored to what once was—absolute power for the granter."

"Oh, my! What did she say?"

"She snorted in his face and dismissed him."

"Lucabara, if we're going to keep the war from starting, we have to do something fast."

"Fine. But how?"

Perloo thought for a moment. Then, rather sadly, he said, "I don't know."

Lucabara took out the proclamation half from her smock. "If we could match this up with the other part," she said, "and show it to the tribe, they would know Berwig isn't granter."

"I suppose."

"But that," continued Lucabara, "means escaping from this place, going home, getting the other half of the proclamation, putting it together, and sharing it."

Perloo shook his head. "I can't do it."

"Why?"

"I gave Weyanto my word I wouldn't escape."

"Perloo, they're Felbarts. It doesn't matter what you say to them."

"Lucabara," Perloo said softly, "I like keeping my word."

"What about stopping the war?"

After a moment Perloo said, "If I ever really do become granter, I'll tell you one thing."

"What?"

"I don't think I'd be very good at making decisions alone."

All that sun-glow Perloo kept hoping that Weyanto would send for him and resume their conversation. No word came. The only visitor they had was their jailer, an amiable, toothless old Felbart who informed them that she had been charged with making the Montmers as comfortable as possible. Every so often she came to renew their water, preab and honey. She even presented them with some grilled horsemint root and pickled milkweed, Montmer favorites.

During one of her visits Perloo asked the old jailer if she knew where the packmaster was.

She shook her head. "I'm too unimportant to know of such high doings."

"Perloo," Lucabara said when the jailer had left them. "I've figured out how to escape."

"How?"

"That jailer of ours," Lucabara suggested. "We can easily overpower her. Then it's just a question of finding our way out of the cave."

"But what about my promise not to escape?"

"I think you'd better forget it."

The two argued the question. Aside from his promise, Perloo wanted to wait more. Lucabara felt they must act immediately. Each had good reasons. In the end, they compromised. Perloo asked for another moon-glow of patience. If, by the early, no word from the packmaster came, he agreed he would try and escape.

BERWIG THE GRANTER

CHAPTER 20

"DO I LOOK powerful?" Berwig asked, straining to
see a reflection of himself in a small, paw-held mica
mirror. "Am I too ferocious?" He and Senyous were
just outside the Great Hall in the Central Tribe
Burrow. Berwig was wearing his best golden wolf fur
smock, his whiskers had been brushed to brilliance,
his ear tips had been beeswaxed to barbed points, and
his round cheeks glowed with buffalo grease.

Not far from them stood a troop of twenty
Montmer warriors. Each wore wooden armor. Pikes,
tipped with thorns, were in their paws.

"May I humbly urge you to straighten your
smock," Senyous said. He was holding Jolaine's rewritten proclamation.

Though annoyed, Berwig did as told, then stole a
scratch.

"And if, oh, Granter, you could keep from scratching," Senyous added, "it would add to your grandeur."

"Stop telling me what to do!" Berwig snapped.
"You seem to keep forgetting that I'm the granter."

Senyous abased himself with a low bow. "Of course

it is you who are granter," he whispered through clenched teeth. "How could I ever forget that? May I offer you the proclamation?"

Berwig snatched it from Senyous's paws.

"Gently!" Senyous shrieked. "It's fragile. I worked very hard!"

"Never mind *your* work. Let's get on with mine," Berwig growled.

Senyous took a deep breath to calm himself. "If I may be so bold, Granter, when you read from the proclamation, try to keep your paws from trembling. Make the effort to look like a granter."

"Are you suggesting I'm not one?" Berwig said.

"I'm suggesting nothing," Senyous said with another low bow that concealed a smirk. "I assure you, Granter, all you need do is show yourself on the field of battle, and the Felbarts will race away. You are, oh, Granter, perfectly savage in your appearance.

"And I promise," Senyous continued, "when you return from the war I—who, alas, must stay behind—will arrange a great triumph."

Berwig, saying nothing, only stole another look in the mirror and adjusted a whisker strand.

Senyous offered Berwig another leaf of bark. "Here is the speech I wrote for you," he said.

Berwig flung it aside. "I can give my own speeches, thank you. And they're a lot better than yours."

Muttering venomous oaths under his breath, Senyous approached the warriors. A burly fellow with scarred face and ears was the commander.

"March them in," Senyous snapped.

The commander pulled a ragged ear, turned to his troops and shouted, "Start beating . . . now!"

The warriors lifted their pikes and smote them against their wooden armor in unison. The result was a sharp, rhythmic *clack*, which, when made by all the soldiers and repeated steadily, reverberated through the halls.

"Begin to go forward—hop!" the commander called.

Beating their pikes, the warriors began to hop up and down in place. This they did in alternate rows, so that while half jumped up the other half held their ground until the first half landed. Then the second half jumped while the first half paused. Up and down they went, creating a wave-like effect. At a predetermined count, they all began to hop forward into the Great Hall.

Berwig, all but tripping on his smock, trying to keep from scratching himself, moved to the rear of his troops. As the last row moved forward, he hopped along with them. Senyous entered the Great Hall too but kept himself apart.

The hall was packed with Montmers straining and gawking to see the warriors. As the soldiers entered the hall, Gumpel, hidden midst the crowd, shouted, "Hurrah, for our warriors!"

None of the Montmers took up the cry, but when Gumpel altered her words to, "Hurrah for Montmers," the cheer was taken up by a few and then, in a listless tone, by the whole crowd.

Following the bawled orders of their commander, the warriors split into two equal sections, one to each side of the Settop. There, with a final clack, they stopped.

Berwig tried to keep in step with them. Once, twice, he adjusted his hop only to stumble. Each time he almost fell, bringing a gasp from some of the on-lookers, snorts from others. Managing to right himself, he continued on.

When Berwig came to the Settop he halted. Puffing up his cheeks, stroking his whiskers—while trying to conceal an occasional scratch—he tried to look as ferocious as possible.

Directly behind the Settop were four musicians with sounders, which made a sound not unlike the braying of elk. As soon as Berwig took his position, they lifted them to their lips and began to blow. Berwig waited impatiently.

When the music was over Berwig lifted the proclamation in paws so trembling the bark fairly rattled.

"As your, hmm, granter," he began, "it's my obligation to . . . ah, bring you, well, important news. And the news is actually, bad. I have learned that the Felbarts, because of the, uh, bad weather, have—" unable to restrain himself, he scratched his neck "—come on to our territory."

There was an angry murmur from the crowd.

"As your granter, the peerless power in our land,

you can be sure that I'll . . . well . . . lead my invincible warriors to, I guess, repel every attack. Moreover, when I, along with my . . . hmmm . . . mighty warriors —have beaten them back, I'll advance upon them, and destroy them a lot and, uh, take back all the lands they . . . well, took from us . . . me."

The Montmers in the hall stared intently at Berwig. A few rolled their eyes.

"But, well, unfortunately," Berwig continued, "I must also tell you, that there are some Montmers who are aiding our . . . enemies."

"No! Not possible!" was heard from the crowd.

"As you know, my mother, the, ah, sainted Jolaine of recent memory, was murdered by . . . Perloo. He was helped by Lucabara. These two—through some bad treachery—escaped from the Central Tribal Burrow and, actually, I think they've gone, you know, over to the Felbart side." He scratched his nose.

"If you have any, hmmm, doubts about Perloo, I'll share Jolaine's last proclamation. Listen to what . . . well . . . she thought of Perloo."

Clearing his throat Berwig read the rewritten proclamation.

The reaction of the crowd was mixed. Some expressed anger. Other shook their heads in disbelief. Most simply took in the news as if not sure what to do or say.

Berwig looked around and said, "You are all . . . uh

free to, hmmm, inspect this document. I'll have some-one fix it to the wall.

"Are there any, well, questions?" he asked. "Does any one wish to defend Perloo? Any one want to question this document? Or . . . say anything?"

A young Montmer by the name of Quitpo hopped out of the crowd. "How do we know that Jolaine's proclamation is real?" he called.

The boldness of the question so surprised Berwig he could do little more than gawk at the fellow. His trembling increased. His itchiness became awful.

It was Senyous who took action. He jumped for-ward and stared up at Quitpo. "Is it possible that you're calling Granter Berwig a *liar*?" he hissed.

"No, not at all," Quitpo said. "I'm merely asking—"

"Are you defending Perloo?" Senyous interrupted, his voice rising to a shriek. "Supporting the Felbarts? Encouraging our enemies? Defending traitors?"

"Of course not. It's just . . ."

Senyous whirled about. "Arrest this traitor!" he cried to the military commander. "Quickly!"

The commander and two warriors hopped for-ward, and before the protester could say another word, he was dragged from the great hall, crying, "I was only asking a—"The doors slammed on him.

It all happened so quickly none of the onlookers in the hall did a thing.

Senyous bowed low before Berwig. "Did you wish to say anything more, oh, Granter?"

"Me? Uh . . . no," a thoroughly rattled Berwig replied. "That's fine. I'm done."

From the back of the hall, Gumpel cried out, "Death to Perloo! Death to all traitors!"

Slowly but surely, the cry was taken up by others.

Berwig snorted with relief. He was, he told himself, really wonderful. And brave. Full of himself, he hopped out of the hall.

The crowd, buzzing with excitement, gathered around the posted proclamation. In the middle of the crowd was Gumpel.

"How curious," she said to herself after reading the proclamation a few times. "It denounces Perloo, but says nothing about who is to become the new granter."

For a long time Gumpel stared at the proclamation. The more she looked at it, the more certain she was she saw a jagged seam running the length of the proclamation. "Two sheets," she concluded. "Glued. I wonder where the other half is. And what it said."

Quitting the Great Hall, Gumpel hopped to Berwig's room. The granter, recovering from his ordeal, was on his bed, eating.

"How did I sound?" he asked.

"Thrilling."

"I thought so," Berwig agreed. "Well, what do you want?"

"Will you be leading your army against the Felbarts?"

"I suppose I have to," Berwig replied.

"May I," Gumpel mumbled, "suggest something?"

"If you must."

"Let Senyous march at the head of the army."

Berwig squinted at Gumpel. "That's the granter's place," he growled.

"I suppose," returned Gumpel with a yawn and a few blinks of her bleary eyes. "Of course, it is the most dangerous spot."

Berwig stared at the creature before him. Then he suddenly sucked in his breath. "You know, it might be a good thing to put Senyous up front. It might teach him a lesson. How clever of me to think of that." Suddenly, he frowned. "But, who would remain in charge here?"

"Oh, well," Gumpel replied as if the question had never occurred to her, "perhaps . . . me."

ESCAPE!

WHEN PERLOO WOKE next early he felt uneasy. Since Weyanto had not come, this was the sun-glow he had agreed he and Lucabara would make an attempt to escape. But when he remembered his promise to Weyanto that he wouldn't flee, he could not rid himself of the feeling he was doing something wrong.

Gazing at the picture of Mogwat on the wall, he remembered her saying, "Of all things, the hardest to keep is a promise."

Oh, why, Perloo wondered, have I been agreeing to do so many things I don't want to do? He kept wishing Weyanto would come.

"Ready to escape?" was the first thing Lucabara said when she woke.

"Lucabara," Perloo said, "I think we should be more patient."

"You're the granter," she returned. "I'll listen to your orders."

"Remember what I said?" Perloo grumbled. "It

takes more than one to make a decision now."

"Then I say we should go."

"What about my promise to the packmaster?"

"Did he come?" Lucabara asked.

Perloo sighed. "No."

"It won't be hard," said Lucabara, who had been working on a scheme. "First we'll make the light a little dimmer. That'll make it difficult for anyone to see us. You'll sit facing the door. Act as if you're asleep. I'll be *behind* the door. When our jailer comes in, I'll knock her down. Soon as she's down, you hop out the door. I'll be right behind. It's that easy."

"She's done us no harm," Perloo said ruefully.

"She's a Felbart."

Perloo shook his head. "To tell the truth, they don't seem to be very different than us."

"Do you wish to escape or not?" Lucabara asked.

Perloo sighed. "I'll go," he said. "But how do you expect to get out of the cave?"

"It's huge. Sooner or later we'll find an exit."

"It better be sooner," Perloo murmured. "Do you have Jolaine's proclamation?"

Lucabara touched her smock. "Right here."

They made their preparations. Lucabara blew out all but one of the candles, making the room dim. Perloo took his place directly opposite the entryway. Lucabara squatted behind the door.

Perloo was very tense. "This isn't right," he kept muttering to himself as he fussed with his whiskers, "it just isn't."

After a long wait they heard steps coming from outside the door.

"Ready!" Lucabara whispered.

Perloo pressed his back against the wall but shut his eyes only partially. He wanted to see what happened. The door swung open. The Felbart at the door hesitated at the threshold before coming further into the room.

Lucabara leaped, high enough for her to come down on the Felbart's back with the full force of both her long feet.

Taken by surprise, the Felbart let forth an "oomph!" and collapsed before Perloo's feet. He gasped with horror. It was not their jailer, but Packmaster Weyanto.

"Perloo," Lucabara shouted. "Hop it!"

"But . . . it's the packmaster," Perloo cried.

Lucabara faltered. "I'm sorry," she said. "But he shouldn't have been so sneaky. Anyway, it's too late. We've got to move!"

But Perloo could not move. For all he knew Weyanto was dead. "I knew something bad would happen," he groaned.

"Hurry!" Lucabara cried and pulled him away. Not knowing what to do, Perloo allowed himself to be led.

The cave corridors were gloomy. Only a few wall candles were burning. Lucabara kept pulling Perloo forward. Then, as they went around a corner they all but crashed into their jailer. She was on her way to the cell with food. Startled, the three stopped and stared at one another. It was the jailer who moved first, turning and rushing off. "Escape!" she howled. "The Montmers have escaped!"

As fast as they could, Lucabara and Perloo hopped in the opposite direction, going through one corridor after another. A breathless Perloo found it hard to keep up.

"This way," Lucabara kept shouting. "Faster!" She made a sharp turn into a dark area, one which looked —as far as Perloo could see—as if it were littered with rock and stone debris. Lucabara halted and squatted down.

"Look!" she said in a whisper.

Not far off was a pair of large wooden doors. Two Felbart guards—bone clubs in hand—were marching up and down before them.

"There!" Lucabara said with excited but muted satisfaction. "A way out."

"Lucabara," Perloo whispered, "we've made a dreadful mistake. We're supposed to be keeping the peace, not starting the war! I think we've killed Weyanto."

Paying Perloo no heed, Lucabara turned to study the doors. As she watched four warriors came racing down the same tunnel through which they had just passed.

"The Montmers!" barked one of the newcomers to those guarding the door. "They attacked the pack-master and escaped from their cell."

"Was he hurt?" one of the guards asked.

"I'm not sure. Be doubly on the watch! We must catch them!" The four newcomers raced away.

"Lucabara!" Perloo cried. "We really . . ."

"Shhh! Keep down!"

From midst the rubble at their feet she selected a small stone, picked it up, and flung it in a high arc so that it landed on the far side of the door.

At the noise the guards whirled. "What was that?" cried one of them. Waiting for another sound, they held their clubs in readiness.

Lucabara picked up another stone and tossed it a little farther than her first.

"There!" one of the guards said. "That way." They began to creep forward—away from the door.

Lucabara threw two more stones, each a greater distance from the door than before. She was leading the guards away.

"Ready," she cautioned as she threw one more stone.

The guards moved still further away.

"Now!" Lucabara urged. At the word she and Perloo began to hop toward the doors. The guards heard and saw them. "Halt! Stop!" they cried and started after them.

Lucabara had planned her move perfectly. By the time the Felbarts realized what was happening, she and Perloo were at the doors. She yanked them open and hopped out of the cave.

Perloo, however, did not go. Lucabara took a dozen

hops before she realized it. When she did, she spun about. "Perloo!" she cried. "What are you doing?"

"I've got to do things my way," he called to her. "I'm going to stay. Go and try and stop the war."

"Perloo!" she shouted.

But by then the door guards had knocked Perloo down, and slammed the door shut.

LUCABARA

"OH, PERLOO," LUCABARA cried in vexation, "why must you be so foolish?"

She took two hops in the direction of the cave only to stop, realizing there was nothing she could do to help him now. In haste she hopped off until she knew she was safe. Then she paused and looked down the mountain. Where should she go? If she returned home and was caught by Berwig and Senyous, she had little doubt as to her fate.

She could flee into exile to some other part of the mountain, perhaps to another mountain entirely. There were other Montmer tribes. No doubt she could find some kind of life for herself.

Or perhaps she should stay and work secretly to lead a rebellion.

But what about the war with the Felbarts? She felt she owed it to the tribe to try to stop it. In the end it might be the best way—the only way—to help Perloo.

Then, she asked herself, did she really want to help Perloo? All she had done so far was out of loyalty to

Jolaine, not Perloo. Indeed, when Jolaine had first told her about Perloo, Lucabara had been disappointed. What had Jolaine called him? "Perloo the Unwilling."

Lucabara looked up and about. It was a little past sun-up. The sun was low to the east. The great blizzard had ended the previous night. Before her, in profound stillness, beneath seamless mounds of powdered snow, lay the land. Above, the sky was a brilliant, cloudless blue. Every tree—every pine needle—was coated with ice as delicate as a porcupine quill. Though the air was crystal clear, she could almost taste it. It made her want to fly away.

She did the next best thing. Knees flexed, leaning slightly forward, ears back, stubby arms tucked in, she sped down the mountain like an avalanche, allowing her whole body to feel the thrill of plunging speeds that made her spirits soar. Was there anything better than skiing!

Then she made herself move slowly, skiing long, looping patterns. The steady rhythmic swaying of her body, the graceful flow and sweep of movement, the spray of powder in her face, soothed her troubled spirits while the whispering slide of her feet sounded a steady hiss that was like a song in her ears. How she loved the speed, the sensation of being in complete control. It was as if she were racing along the very edge of life.

Then, as she swept out from behind a ridge, the full range of mountains opened up before her in one vast, horizon-filling panorama. Quickly, Lucabara shifted her feet so that their sides bit deep into the snow. It brought her to a quick, snow-spraying stop.

The view before Lucabara, snow crowned majestic peak after snow crowned majestic peak, randomly necklaced with jagged black outcroppings against intense blue skies, seemed to go on forever. Moved by the great beauty she stretched out her short arms as if to hug all the mountains. "Oh," she cried, "this is my world and I love it!" With her cry came renewed strength. She felt full of hope.

Yes, she felt she must assist her Montmer tribe. And Perloo? He was not very bold, powerful, or even romantic. Not her notion of a granter.

On the other paw, she had to acknowledge he did keep his promises, was smart and loyal. Decent too. Nice, and kind. Most of all, he didn't pretend to be anything more than what he was. How like him not to escape! Lucabara forced herself to admit there was a kind of bravery in that. Yes, Perloo was what he was. No more, but no less either. Was not that the kind of leadership the Montmers needed? Could that have been what Jolaine saw in Perloo? A Montmer who—because of his knowledge and modesty—would expand their freedoms.

Just to say it made her realize that of course it was!

Suddenly Lucabara saw that the best way to help the Montmers was to make sure Perloo stayed alive so he could become granter. Jolaine was the past. Perloo was the future.

Resolute, Lucabara began to ski hard down the mountain.

By middle sun-glow she began to recognize the familiar landmarks of Montmer territory. Once she came upon wolf tracks. Twice she saw mountain goats. But nervous only about warrior patrols, she skied slowly.

Her watchfulness was rewarded. From a distance she spied a squad of warriors skiing in line. A military patrol!

Moving quickly, she skied into a clump of pine trees and hid herself while observing what they did.

The squad, six in number, was dressed in full military armor and were armed with pikes. She saw them approach a burrow mound and knock upon its top entrance. When the door opened, she watched as they pushed down and disappeared below.

Apprehensive, Lucabara waited.

The patrol soon returned to the surface. With them were two struggling Montmers—arms bound behind their backs—who were being led away as prisoners. Behind them, at the burrow entrance, two anguished Montmers looked on.

As soon as the patrol was out of sight, Lucabara skied to the burrow. The two Montmers were still there, weeping.

"What's happened?" Lucabara called.

"It's Senyous's patrols. They've taken two from the burrow."

"But . . . why?"

"The same as elsewhere," one of the Montmers wept. "They objected to Berwig."

"And Senyous," added the other.

"What will they do with them?" Lucabara called.

"Don't you know, they've turned the Central Tribe Burrow into a huge prison."

"Oh," cried the second, "the day Jolaine died was a doleful day for all of us!"

Consoling one another the two hopped down into their burrow, slamming the door behind them.

Lucabara, angry and upset, skied away. The situation had become much worse than she would have thought possible in such a short time. She had to find a hiding place quickly, somewhere to plan a rebellion. Her own home—the Central Tribe Burrow—was impossible. She would have to go to friends. But who among them could she trust, or for that matter, put into jeopardy with her presence?

She thought of any number, but settled on one Rembury, a young female Montmer with whom she had enjoyed skiing. Lucabara was certain she could trust her. And Rembury lived near Tupthang Hollow, not far from where she was.

Keeping a careful watch, making certain of escape routes should she run into a patrol, Lucabara made her way. Twice she found evidence that patrols had passed recently; the trails of six skiers moving in close formation. She pushed on.

Tupthang Hollow was nestled in a small valley surrounded by rocky fields. With the rocks buried deep in the snow, access was easy.

Lucabara took the time to make sure no one was watching her. Only then did she approach and pound on the door. It was not long before she heard the sound of someone hopping up the tunnel. The peephole opened. Quickly, she set herself close against the door, so only the tips of her ears could be seen.

"Share your name!" came a request from within.

"I'm looking for Rembury," Lucabara said, avoiding using her own name.

The door dropped open. Rembury herself popped out. "Lucabara!" she cried with a mix of alarm and delight. "Where have you been?"

Rembury was a strong, young, muscular Montmer, with a famously flashing smile and long hair tuft—dyed green—the kind that passed for fashion among young female Montmers. She had a way of setting her ears at a particular rakish angle that had always appealed to Lucabara as wonderfully bold.

Not waiting for an invitation, Lucabara hopped into the burrow entryway. Rembury pushed the door up behind her.

"By Mogwat, Lucabara," Rembury said, "did you know Berwig and his warriors have been looking for you and that Perloo everywhere? They've accused you of murdering Jolaine."

"Would you rather I not stop?" Lucabara asked.

"No, of course not. You, murder Jolaine? Impossible! And I know all about Berwig and Senyous."

"What about your burrowmates?" Lucabara asked.

"You don't have to worry," Rembury assured her. "We've got sixteen here and most of us have the good sense to know what's going on. But I should warn you, warrior patrols have been making sudden search and grabs."

"I saw it happen."

Rembury shook her head. "They're picking up anyone who opposes Berwig's rule. But they've not come here. Not yet anyway. You can hide in my burrow room."

Leading the way, Rembury hopped down the tunnel. Before coming to the main hall, she turned into a small side tunnel, then another before entering her burrow room. It was small, snug, and very neat, with a glowing fire. Once there she shut the door and urged Lucabara to rest.

As Rembury scurried about getting some food, Lucabara told the story of Jolaine, Berwig, and Perloo. When she was done Rembury could only murmur, "Awful, just awful."

As Lucabara ate and drank some tea, Rembury, having good Montmer manners, remained silent. But once she had her fill, Lucabara said, "As far as I know, Perloo is still up there with the Felbarts. Rembury, I'm just hoping he gets out alive."

Rembury—eyes twinkling—considered Lucabara with interest. "You care for him a lot, don't you?"

Lucabara, her nose turning a deep purple, smiled shyly.

"Don't worry," Rembury said. "It sounds like he knows what he's doing. Tell me again what happened to your part of Jolaine's proclamation?"

Lucabara reached into her smock and drew it out. Rembury examined it only to shake her head. "Doesn't make any sense," she said.

"I helped Jolaine write it so I can tell you what the other half said."

"I'm listening."

Lucabara recited it for her.

When Lucabara had done, Rembury said, "You do know, don't you, that Berwig and Senyous have another version of Jolaine's proclamation? It condemns Perloo."

"Rembury, believe me, it must be a forgery."

"I'm only telling you what I saw."

"But I need to know," Lucabara said, "if you heard anything about a war."

Rembury looked grim. "The rumor is the Felbarts are going to attack."

"Another lie," Lucabara informed her friend, and told Rembury about the letter Berwig sent to the Felbarts. She also recounted the story of Granter Wentlow.

Rembury snorted. "I never thought you were a student of history."

Lucabara's nose turned purple again. "I'm not. Perloo told me about him. Rembury," she asked, "can

I meet with some of your friends? Would they be willing to listen to me, talk with me? We need to organize fast."

"I'll see who I can round up."

Lucabara, remaining alone, squatted down before the fire, sipped some tea, and thought about what Rembury had told her. At least there was *some* resistance to Berwig. If only she could help to shape it, direct it. Lucabara folded the proclamation and returned it to her smock.

Rembury soon returned, bringing five of her burrowmates with her.

"Lucabara here, has something to tell us," Rembury said, introducing her mates to Lucabara. "Listen to her, then feel free to ask questions."

The five Montmers squatted down. Starting with Jolaine's rejection of Berwig as new granter, Lucabara began to tell the entire story.

She had barely told half the tale when there was a sudden pounding on Rembury's door.

"Open up," barked a voice. "Warrior patrol!"

THE NEW GRANTER

AS SOON AS SENYOUS was informed that the great blizzard was over, he assembled an army of one hundred Montmer warriors. In full armor, pikes in paw, they lined up in the Great Hall, awaiting the arrival of Berwig. Crowds of nervous onlookers pressed against the walls to watch.

While the warriors were stiff and stone-faced, their toes curled with tension, the spectators were full of emotion. Excitement, pride, worry, fear, and indignation—all were there.

Midst the onlookers was Gumpel, acting bored. No one paid her any mind.

Senyous, however, was hopping up and down before the warriors, issuing orders, reminding them of the battle plan. "Remember all I've taught you about how and where to fight," he told them. "If you do you can't lose."

Senyous's thoughts contradicted his words. It was his expectation that just before hopping off at the head of the army, Berwig would appoint him acting-granter. Then, while the army and Berwig were gone, he, Senyous would secure his own power. Key to his plan were two hopes: the defeat of the Montmer army by the Felbarts, and Berwig's death on the battlefield.

Of course, there was always the chance the Felbarts might then really attack. What did Senyous care? He would deal with that later—if he had to. When he was granter.

The doors of the Great Hall swung open. Four musicians with sounders hopped in. Putting horns to mouths they blew braying fanfares. It was the cue for Berwig's entry. In he hopped, bulky in a red fox fur smock, ears beeswaxed to perfect points, newly dyed whiskers swept back in an attitude of ferocity. In one paw he held a pike adorned with dragonfly wings.

"Salute Granter Berwig!" Senyous cried.

As one, the warriors grasped their left ears and chanted, "Great Ho to the granter! Great Ho to the granter!" after which they beat their wooden armor with their pikes.

Accepting the salute with a gleeful, gapped-tooth grin, Berwig took a few pompous hops in front of the troops, pausing occasionally to scratch himself.

"Oh, Granter," Senyous said in a loud voice when Berwig settled himself upon the Settop, "as your first assistant I have the honor of presenting your mighty army to you. Your loyal warriors are ready, willing, and able to die in the defense of your honor and the honor of our tribal territory. Is that not true?" he added, turning to the warriors.

"Ho!" they cried as one while clacking their armor.

"Ho for our army!" Gumpel shouted out from midst the crowd. A goodly number in the crowd, swept up by the excitement, repeated the cheer.

Berwig pulled himself up as tall as he was capable, placed one paw upon his heart, and squinted at the troops. "Montmer warriors!" he bellowed, "with your help, I, hmmm . . . am about to go and . . . well, defend the homelands from, uh, the stupid aggression of our ancient enemies, the Felbarts. Fear not. I, Berwig the Big shall, ah, lead you to, well, glory. Nothing shall, uh, deter us from, actually, victory."

"Prepare to hop!" Senyous ordered the troops.

As one the troops clacked their armor.

"Stop!" Berwig suddenly cried. "I have another important announcement to make."

Senyous, anticipating that Berwig was about to proclaim him acting-granter, made an effort to look humble.

Berwig continued. "I . . . uh . . . need to inform my subjects about who's going to be in charge while I'm away winning this war."

Senyous crept forward, the better to accept Berwig's transfer of power to him in as modest a manner as he could manage.

"Because," Berwig continued, "he has been of such a help and, actually, support to me, I have decided to honor my first assistant, Senyous, by allowing him—"

Berwig turned toward Senyous, smirked, then said, "to come along with us!"

Flabbergasted, Senyous stared openmouthed at Berwig.

"The fact is, Senyous is so eager to show his bravery I've decided to place him in the command position at the head of the army. Senyous, hop forward and accept your great honor."

Furious, but forced to hide his emotions, Senyous approached Berwig. "What are you doing, you fool!" he snarled in a low voice. "I'm supposed to stay here and make sure all will be in order for your triumphant return!"

"You're coming with me," Berwig returned. "What's more you're going to hop at the front of the army so I can keep you in sight."

"I won't do it!"

"You will or I'll dismiss you on the spot," Berwig snarled. "Make up your mind!"

Senyous stared at Berwig. He did not think Berwig was capable of living up to his threat, but this was not, he decided, the moment to act. "Fool," he hissed to Berwig, but said no more.

Delighted with his success, Berwig cried out in a loud voice, "Senyous, with . . . uh . . . great affection I present you with the dragonfly pike as a token of the trust I have in you!"

So saying he handed the pike to Senyous, who, having little choice, took it. For a fleeting moment Senyous was tempted to spike Berwig with it. Again, he resisted the temptation. "In time," he told himself, and held his paw.

"And who do you think is going to manage things here for you while we're away?" he asked in an undertone.

"I've got the perfect one," retorted Berwig.

"Who?" Senyous yelped.

Berwig turned and addressed the crowd. "Gumpel, please come forward!"

Gumpel, squat and rumpled, bleary eyes blinking, hopped toward Berwig with a great show of reluctance. All around her Montmers shifted nervously to let her—and her foul odor—pass.

Approaching Berwig, she bowed low to the floor.

Senyous's ears shook with rage.

At the depth of her bow, Gumpel pulled her left ear and muttered, "Oh, Granter, I am surprised and humbled by this honor."

"I should think you would be," Berwig agreed. "Now then, Gumpel, I want your promise that you'll keep things in perfect order, making sure that you will, you know, uphold justice, honor, and all that rubbish."

"Of course," Gumpel murmured. "I won't think of doing anything else."

"Good. Fine. We'll be back as soon as I rout the Felbarts. Senyous, take your place at the head of the army and lead us away."

Bursting with rage, Senyous hopped forward. "Prepare to hop!" he snarled.

The Montmer army began to hop up and down. "Ready, hop!" the commanders cried. Clacking their armor, the warriors began to hop out of the Great Hall in lines of three. Senyous—ears twitching with rage—was at the head.

Berwig followed the last of the warriors out of the hall even as the musicians gave one final bleat on their sounders.

The doors to the Great Hall were shut. All became still save for the diminishing sound of the clacking army.

For a long while Gumpel remained staring at the closed doors. Then she turned. Everyone in the Great Hall was staring at her.

Blinking, nodding, Gumpel hopped slowly toward the Settop. When she came close to it she paused, put out a paw, and stroked its surface gently.

Trembling with excitement, she sat down, wiggling to place herself just right. When she was firmly seated she looked up at the crowd. "Very well then," she sighed in her sleepy drawl, "I am the . . . granter." She smiled slyly. "From now on everyone must do what *I* want."

CAPTURED

WHEN THE MONTMER warrior patrol banged on the door of Rembury's burrow room, she and her five friends, as well as Lucabara, were taken completely by surprise.

"Let us in!" a voice demanded. "By order of Granter Berwig."

"Share your name!" Rembury said, stalling for time.

"Commander Tonlow, on conspiracy service!"

Within the room all eyes went to Lucabara. "Don't give them my name," she begged in a whisper. "That's all I ask."

"Don't worry," Rembury said as she got up and opened the door.

A stern-faced Montmer commander, in full armor, ears quivering with aggression, stood on the threshold. Another warrior, holding a sheet of bark, stood by his side. Four other warriors, armed with thorn pikes, peered into the room.

"What do you want?" Rembury asked.

"We're looking for traitors," the commander snarled.

"There are only loyal tribe members here," Rembury replied.

The commander eyed the room's occupants with suspicion. "What's your name?" he demanded abruptly, pointing to a fellow with tall, thin ears, possum fur smock, and trembling paws.

"Bis . . . wicker," the Montmer stammered.

The commander turned to the warrior with a bark sheet. " 'Biswicker,' he said. Is he on the list?"

Mumbling names to herself as she ran a paw down a long list, the warrior suddenly stopped, and jabbed the bark. "*Biswicker.* Right here."

"All right then," the commander said to the frightened Biswicker, "hop on out."

"But . . . why?" the poor fellow cried.

"You're under arrest for making a disparaging remark about the granter's itching."

"But . . . anyone can *say* things."

"I'm not here to argue, fellow. You're on the list First Assistant Senyous drew up. That's all I need to know."

The four armed warriors hopped into the room. Rembury's friends, including Lucabara, moved as one to block the way to the cringing Biswicker.

"You can't take him!" Rembury cried. "You have no right."

"Now look here," the commander shouted. "I'm warning you all. I've got orders that if there's any resistance to the taking of traitors I'm to arrest all obstructionists! As far as I'm concerned you're all thwarting me. Now, last chance. Hop aside."

No one moved.

The four warriors lowered their sharp pikes, aimed them directly at those shielding Biswicker, and lurched forward. One of the warriors pricked Rembury's arm. She gave a yelp, clutched her arm, and fell back over Biswicker. The others, fearing for their lives, scrambled away.

"The rest of you are under arrest!" ordered the commander. "Now hop on out!" he cried.

With Rembury wounded, those who had remained in the room—including Lucabara—were quickly marched through the burrow at pike's point.

Trying to hide her agitation, Lucabara felt for the proclamation beneath her smock. It was safe.

As they made their way through the tunnels, the other burrow inhabitants peeked fearfully out from behind partially open doors. No one attempted a rescue.

Once outside, the prisoners were lined up in single file. Lucabara stayed close to Rembury, who was clutching her arm.

The patrol, with its line of prisoners, skied to the Central Tribe Burrow. As Lucabara moved along, she kept wondering how long it would take before she was recognized. After all, the Central Tribe Burrow was her home. Many residents could and would recognize her on sight. Grimly, she made up her mind. If she was identified she'd attempt to flee—no matter what the consequences.

But the patrol did not use the main entrance. Instead, the commander chose an ancient bolt hole, one rarely used. It led almost directly into the lower regions of the burrow. Lucabara's guess was that Berwig and Senyous did not want the arrests to be known.

The prisoners were herded into a small, dim, wood-lined jail room. Lucabara recognized it instantly as the one in which Perloo had been placed when Berwig first held him. As they were going in she called out, "What about someone to look at Rembury's wound?"

"We've got better things to do," the warrior replied.

The jail door was slammed shut, an outside latch drawn.

Though small, the room was not empty. Twelve other prisoners were already there. Disheveled, bleary eyed, smocks dirty, they were a downcast, hungry-looking lot.

Lucabara recognized some of them as living in the Central Tribe Burrow. In one corner, partially withdrawn into his smock, she spotted Chef Fergink. Despondent, he barely looked up at the newcomers. Lucabara wondered how long it would be before he —or someone else—recognized her.

The prisoners began to exchange stories as to why and how they had been arrested. While tales varied, all shared one thing in common: Each had objected to Berwig's rule.

"How many do you think have been taken prisoner?" Lucabara asked.

"Can't say," replied one of the prisoners. "They've been doing it since Berwig sat on the Settop. They say it's Senyous's doing."

"But how many?" Lucabara persisted.

"Forty, fifty . . ." someone suggested.

"What about the army?" she asked. "Are the warriors supporting Berwig?"

"Most of them have hopped off to war against the Felbarts."

Lucabara's stomach tumbled. "Has that begun?" she asked.

"One of our guards told us the army left this early."

"Senyous and Berwig went with it," another prisoner added.

"Has anyone been left in charge?" Lucabara asked.

"Gumpel," Chef Fergink snorted.

"Gumpel! But why her?"

From across the cell Chef Fergink suddenly called, "Wait a minute! I know you! You're Lucabara. Jolaine's first assistant. The one I helped escape."

"Oh, my!" cried another. "Jolaine's murderer!"

"It's not true," Lucabara said quickly. "That's all Senyous's and Berwig's lies."

Lucabara told her fellow prisoners about Jolaine's

decision to proclaim Perloo granter in place of
Berwig. To prove her point she took out the piece of
Jolaine's proclamation.

The prisoners studied the torn sheet intensely. One
of them said, "It looks like Jolaine's paw, but it doesn't
make any sense."

"And anyway," another said, "if this Perloo is the
real granter, where is he?"

Lucabara said, "With the Felbarts."

Her reply brought more questions. "What's Perloo
doing with the Felbarts? Has he gone over to their
side? *Did* he murder Jolaine? How come Jolaine
picked him?"

Lucabara answered their questions patiently. Even
so there was considerable debate. Slowly but surely
she convinced them.

It was Chef Fergink who summed up the general
feeling. "Lucabara warned me what would happen
about Berwig. She was right. He's no good. I'm squatting with her."

No one disagreed.

Exhausted with all her talking, and distressed by
the news of the war, Lucabara went off by herself into
one of the corners of the room. Once there she tried
to envision exactly where they were.

As far as she could recall they were at the bottom
of the burrow in a room flanked by two other jail
cells. All three cells—she supposed—were filled with
prisoners. But the more she thought about that, the
more an idea filled her mind. If there *were* fifty

prisoners, if they could band together, get out of the cell, and become armed, perhaps they *could* do something.

The main thing was to get together.

Lucabara reached around and poked at the wood paneling. There was no way she could get behind it—not by herself, but if others helped. . . .

She hopped over to Rembury.

"Rembury," she said softly, "there may be a way to do something."

Rembury shrugged. "I'm all for that," she said. "But how?"

"The wood paneling is to keep us from burrowing out. But these cells were meant for two prisoners. There are enough of us that we all might pry the wood out. Once we did we could get to the earth behind and burrow."

"Where would that get us?" Rembury asked.

"To either side of us are other cells. I'll bet they're full of prisoners too. If we could join up, we could overpower any guards that walked in."

"And then?"

"Rembury, I was first assistant to Jolaine. I know all the burrow's secret places. I know where the pike room is—where all the army's pikes are stored. Once we're armed, there will be no stopping us."

PERLOO AMONG THE FELBARTS

THOUGH PERLOO WAS hardly surprised when the Felbart guards grabbed him, he was not prepared to be knocked down, dragged through the den with great harshness, and flung into a small, dismal cell, hardly more than a black hole in the rock.

As the guards left he called out, "Please! I need to speak to someone. Is the packmaster all right? I want to make an apology!"

Barking in mockery, the warriors shut the door and latched it.

Perloo sighed. He may have been a Felbart prisoner before, but he had not felt like one. This time he felt very much the criminal.

It was a long sun-glow. Perloo spent much of the first part thinking on the heroic doings of his favorite ancient Montmer heroes. But in the midst of his reflections he suddenly recalled one of Mogwat's sayings, "They who pine for the past, fear the future." "She was right," Perloo reflected. "This isn't the time to be mulling over the past. It's *now* I have to deal with!"

It was while rehearsing an apology speech he hoped to make to the Felbarts, that his cell door was flung open. Two Felbart warriors ordered Perloo to get up. "You're wanted," they informed him.

"By whom? Where?" Perloo asked nervously. "Is Weyanto all right?"

"Do as you're told," was the barked reply.

After attaching ropes to his arms and legs, the Felbarts led Perloo to a large room whose size reminded him of the Great Hall in the Central Tribe Burrow. Waiting at the far end was Packmaster Weyanto. The packmaster was seated upon a low platform. He looked rather the worse for the stomping Lucabara had given him. Sadder too.

Ranged around him were rows of Felbart warriors. All were somber faced, with eyes full of anger, lolling tongues, and flashing fangs as well as tails whipping in great agitation.

As Perloo drew near he pulled down his left ear. "Packmaster, I'm so glad you're—"

"Silence!" Weyanto barked, making it clear that however weak he looked, his voice was in full strength.

"Oh, dry dust," Perloo murmured, afraid to speak.

"Montmer," Weyanto began in a low growl, "though you came to us uninvited, I spoke to you as an equal. I treated you well, hoping we two could keep peace between our tribes.

"When you informed me of your position as granter, I chose to believe your story. I extended much courtesy to you. Then, just as I was coming to talk again, you attacked me and tried to escape. Indeed, your partner did escape. Montmer, before we kill you, do you have anything to say for yourself?"

"Oh, dust," Perloo mumbled. "Very dry dust." He ruffled his scruffy whiskers and worried his paws so much it looked as if he were tying a complicated knot. He tried to look Weyanto in the eye but faltered. "Really, I want to apologize," he managed to say. "You see, you left us alone for so long we had no way of knowing you were coming or what your plans might be. I tried to restrain Lucabara. Then, when she escaped, I decided not to."

"You were captured," Weyanto snapped.

"Well, actually, I could have gotten away," Perloo felt compelled to insist. "I didn't go because I promised I wouldn't. Honestly, if I've learned anything by all this it's that I should only do what I feel is right. And keep my promises," he added sadly.

Weyanto, head cocked to one side, gazed somberly at Perloo. Then he turned to the guards who had captured Perloo at the cave doors. "Is it true what this Montmer says?" he demanded. "Could he have escaped? Or did you keep him from doing it?"

There was some hasty conferring among the Felbart guards. One of them stepped forward. "It's true, Packmaster. He could have gotten away. Instead, he acted as if he wished to remain."

Weyanto's face softened. He turned back to Perloo. "Why did you choose to stay?" he asked. "If you had gone, you might have stopped Berwig's army from attacking us."

"Lucabara went," Perloo replied. "She'll make every effort to stop the war. I remained because I wanted you to trust me."

"You have a curious way of expressing trust," Weyanto said. "Attacking me."

"I was wrong," Perloo said softly.

After a moment Weyanto said, "Do you think your friend can prevent this war?"

"She'll certainly try."

"Then I'm willing—" His words were cut off by a Felbart warrior, fur wet with snow, who burst into the area.

"Packmaster," he cried, "I've just come back from scouting down the mountain. The Montmer army is hopping toward our borders!"

THE MONTMER ARMY ADVANCES

IT WAS MIDDLE sun-glow on Rasquich Mountain and the sun was brilliant in a high blue sky. At a distance the great mountain peaks stood jagged and impenetrable. Overhead a lone eagle circled. The persistent cold air and bright sun had made the snow crusty. The only sound to be heard was that made by the great Montmer army as it hopped along.

Senyous had organized the warriors into two long rows of fifty each. The puffs of their warm breath in the cold air made the army appear like a lumpy caterpillar moving slowly along.

Leading the two lines was Senyous, dragonfly pike in paw. Before him hopped two warriors. One was a scout in charge of following the trail to the Felbart territory. The other—with a pouch over his neck— was map bearer. These two also had the hard work of breaking snow for those who followed.

Senyous had not ceased fuming. How galling, how humiliating, that Berwig had outmaneuvered him! Not only had the granter forced him to come along, he had tricked him into hopping at the head of the army, the most dangerous spot.

The more Senyous thought about it, the more convinced he was that this was not Berwig's thinking. Berwig—he believed—was too stupid for such planning. No, Senyous was sure the scheme had been hatched by Gumpel. As far as Senyous was concerned, the one good thing that resulted from her remaining behind was that Berwig was now helpless.

All the more reason, Senyous thought, to get Berwig quickly killed. Once that was achieved, he, Senyous, would take care of Gumpel. With both Berwig and Gumpel out of the way, nothing could prevent him from becoming granter. Just the thought of it made his nose quiver with excitement.

"Halt!" he cried, lifting a paw. The army came to a ragged stop. "Map bearer!" he shouted.

The map bearer hopped hastily back to Senyous and pulled an ear.

"Show me where we are," Senyous demanded.

The bearer rummaged through his smock and drew out a folded sheet of bark that he offered to Senyous.

"Unfold it, fool!" Senyous said.

The warrior complied.

"Good! In the past, the Felbarts have always constructed a first line of defense, a snow wall, here, on the plain before a canyon. Excellent. We shall attack them there."

"But won't we lose many lives?" the alarmed warrior asked.

"Mind your own business," Senyous snapped. "That's where I want you to lead us."

"But what about the customary first challenge?" asked the warrior.

"We'll let Granter Berwig take care of that. Let *him* be the one to teach the Felbarts a lesson. Once he does the other Felbarts will give way with ease."

"But . . . do you think Granter Berwig can—"

Senyous looked up sharply. "Warrior, are you questioning my strategy?"

"Oh, no, I wouldn't think of it." The map bearer hastily pulled down an ear and hopped back to the other scout and informed him of Senyous's orders. When the second warrior heard of Senyous's plans he darted a concerned look over his shoulder at Senyous but said nothing.

Senyous lifted the dragonfly wing pike. "Move on!" he cried. Once again the army hopped toward Felbart territory.

At the rear of the lines, ten warriors dragged the sledge that carried the army's provisions. Perched atop the sledge, bundled in two smocks as well as extra furs, was Berwig. Two warriors hopped by his side. Their job was to help the granter whenever he slipped and fell, which he did with some frequency.

"I should never have gone to Senyous for advice in the first place," Berwig kept mumbling under his breath. Squinting ahead at the forward lines, he stared at his first assistant malevolently. "Shifty know-it-all," he mumbled. "As if I needed him. I should be home. Being comfortable. Making laws. Punishing those who don't like me. Or," he said with a sigh, "eating. And I will too," he told himself. "As soon as I get rid of Senyous."

He scratched and tried to think up a plan. It had to be a clever one. Senyous was no fool.

Berwig turned to one of the warriors assisting him. "What kind of fighters are these Felbarts, anyway?"

The warrior pulled an ear. "With all due respect, Granter, they can fight pretty well."

"Do they go about fighting in any particular way?" Berwig demanded.

"They don't use pikes, Granter. They use clubs. And teeth. Then there's the usual opening challenge," the warrior explained.

Berwig looked about. "Challenge? What challenge?"

"It's the custom, Granter. When armies meet they offer a challenge—or we do. It's one of our warriors against one of theirs."

"Is that so?"

"If we beat them in the challenge they might just give up. I've seen it happen."

"I see," mused Berwig, scratching himself nervously. "And what happens if they beat us?"

"Pretty much the same. We might as well hop home."

Berwig, seeing an opportunity, began to scheme furiously. If he could fix it so that Senyous was the one to answer the challenge. . . . The thought of Senyous attempting to defend himself with a pike made Berwig snort. He had little doubt Senyous would be killed instantly. Well, perfect! He'd be rid of Senyous and could make an honorable retreat. Exactly what he wanted.

"Here, you," Berwig called to one of his aides. "Go on up ahead and tell Senyous that when we get close to the Felbart borders, we're to make camp for the night."

"Yes, Granter."

"And tell him to make sure I get a good meal. I'm hungry."

THE COMING CHALLENGE

CHAPTER 27

WHEN PERLOO'S INTERVIEW with Weyanto was over, he was led back to his small stone cell more miserable than ever. He began to regret that he had not escaped with Lucabara. He even made a few feeble attempts to scratch at the stone walls and floor, thinking, vaguely, that he might burrow his way out. That proved as futile as his regrets.

As he sat there, growing more and more miserable, he recalled one of Mogwat's sayings: "To resist a challenge is to resist life itself."

What challenge, Perloo asked himself, had he ever accepted? "None," he muttered, all too aware how little he'd done. Perloo recollected another of Mogwat's sayings: "Of all challenges the greatest is to be yourself." I've not even done that, he admitted to himself.

As time slowly passed, Perloo became more and more melancholy. He had even resigned himself to being forgotten when his ears caught the sound of someone approaching. Very quietly, the door was unlatched and opened. It was Weyanto.

The packmaster entered furtively, and shut the door quickly. Perloo jumped to his feet.

Weyanto, his large black eyes full of sorrow, gazed at Perloo. His ears drooped. His tongue lolled. At last he said, "Do you have any idea how difficult you have made things by your foolish attempt at escape? I wish you *had* gotten away."

"What do you mean?" Perloo asked.

"Perloo, I am a peaceful Felbart. Not that I am unwilling to defend myself and my tribe. I assure you I have and I will. I've been to war." He fingered the scar on his snout. "But, if war can be avoided, it must be.

"There are some Felbarts," Weyanto continued, "as I'm sure there are some Montmers—who want this conflict. I'm feeling their pressure. So far your friend has been unable to stop the Montmer army. Perhaps if you had escaped, you might have been more successful."

Perloo fussed with his whiskers but said nothing.

Weyanto scratched himself under his chin meditatively. Then he said, "Perloo, if this war is fought many lives will be lost."

"I'll do anything to prevent it," Perloo said earnestly. "Anything."

Weyanto cocked his head and looked fixedly at him. "Do you mean that?"

"Yes."

"Have you any experience as a warrior?"

Perloo rubbed his paws. "None."

"You've hunted, of course."

"Only a little," Perloo confessed. "I'm best at snow-balls."

The packmaster was not amused by Perloo's attempt at humor. "How do you pass your time?" he wanted to know.

"Reading."

Weyanto growled. "Then you have no experience with the Montmer pike?"

"Very little," Perloo replied.

"I hope you're being modest," the Felbart said gravely.

"Weyanto," Perloo pleaded, "tell me what you have in mind."

"Very well. We Felbarts believe in individual challenges."

"So do Montmers."

"Then you should know that when the Montmer army arrives, Berwig will almost certainly issue a challenge. It is the custom."

"What's that to do with me?" Perloo asked, becoming alarmed.

"Perloo," Weyanto went on, "why should Felbart blood be spilled over a war they did not start or want? You say you will do anything to stop the war from happening. Perhaps," the packmaster went on, "if you were the one to answer Berwig's challenge, the Montmer army might have second thoughts about waging a war against us."

"Me?" Perloo cried in horror. "Fight a challenge?"

"You said you would do anything."

Perloo's stomach began to churn. His knees felt weak. "Packmaster, I've so little experience. Can't you just let me *talk* to my tribe?"

Weyanto snorted. "How you meet the challenge is up to you. But it's you who must accept it."

"Well, yes," Perloo replied in a whisper, "I suppose I understand. And I am willing"—his voice all but faded away—"to try."

"Very well. Come with me. And, Perloo, don't attempt to escape. If you do you will be killed on the spot. In order to do what I've proposed, I had to promise that. Now, come along with me."

Trembling, Perloo followed Weyanto out of the cell. The moment they left it, a squad of Felbart warriors fell in behind.

As they moved through the den Perloo could see just how prepared the Felbarts were. Though not everyone was in armor, virtually all carried bone clubs.

They came into a large, open space that Perloo recognized as the place where he and Lucabara first saw the Felbarts. The stench of meat was intense. Chewed bones lay scattered about. The air was smoky. A large log was blazing, its light reflected on the glistening, teeth-like stalactites. Some fifty Felbart warriors—in armor—were in attendance. All looked grim.

Weyanto moved into the middle of the area, beckoning Perloo to follow. When he did, as if on a pre-arranged signal, the Felbart warriors formed a large circle in which the packmaster and Perloo became the center. Perloo felt the hair at the back of his neck prickle.

"Fellow Felbarts," the packmaster began, addressing his warriors, "as you know the Montmer army is advancing upon us. As you have also been informed, it is being led by Berwig, who claims to be their granter.

"Standing beside me is the Montmer Perloo. He claims to be the true granter, selected by the late Jolaine. Perloo, insisting he is opposed to this war, has promised to do anything to stop it.

"Indeed, he is so against this war, he's willing to put on Felbart armor, take up a Montmer pike—which we captured in the last war—and answer the Montmer challenge that will most surely be given. Hopefully, when his own tribe sees this Montmer opposed to the war, they will retreat peaceably. If not, perhaps he will win the challenge. If he dies, at least it will be a Montmer who falls first in this war brought on by Montmers. What say you to this proposal?"

By way of showing their approval, the warriors lifted their snouts and began to bark, yelp and howl.

Perloo had listened to what Weyanto said as if in a daze. The notion that *he* was to accept a challenge, actually fight someone, filled him with terror. What did he know about fighting? Nothing.

But even as Perloo trembled, two Felbart warriors approached with Felbart armor. It was quickly strapped to his chest, while a helmet was placed over his head, and his ears pulled through the holes. A Montmer pike was thrust into his paw.

The warriors stepped away. When Weyanto backed off Perloo was alone in the center. As the Felbarts appraised him Perloo heard a few muffled snickers.

Weyanto called out, "Salute this Montmer warrior in Felbart armor!"

Barking and yelping reverberated throughout the cave.

Surrounded by Felbart warriors, Perloo was led outside into a deep, narrow canyon. He guessed it was the one into which he and Lucabara had stumbled. The Felbarts had cleared it of snow.

From the canyon they moved onto an opening near the cave. Here, the Felbarts had built a high snow wall. Perloo was marched to the top of the wall. Felbart warriors were prowling about, on the lookout for signs of the advancing Montmer army.

Just before leaving him, Weyanto gazed at Perloo thoughtfully. "Perloo," he said, "have no doubt, a challenge will come. I wish you well." With a whisk of his tail the packmaster went off. As soon as he did a band of Felbart warriors encircled Perloo to prevent escape. There was nothing for Perloo to do but await the challenge.

All that sun-glow Perloo remained atop the Felbart fortifications waiting for the Montmer army to arrive. To pass the time he dozed, daydreamed, or toyed with the pike he'd been issued. When he practiced with it, the Felbart warriors—aware of the coming challenge—watched closely.

At first they were startled by Perloo's inept maneuvers. Then they thought he had developed a technique all his own. But the more they observed the more they realized he was merely incompetent. From then on they watched him only with uneasiness.

"How will I get down from the walls?" Perloo asked one of his guards.

"Don't worry. We have an ice chute that will slide you down."

Perloo tried to remember some Montmer heroes like Lundex the Keen, Buxabec the Brave, and Arkenrol the Deft, famous warriors who had fought notable challenges. All he could think, however, was that it was one thing to have read about history. It's another to *do* history.

To keep his mind off fighting, Perloo tried to compose a speech that he would attempt to give to the Montmer army—assuming he had the opportunity before the fighting began.

The long sun-glow passed without any word of the Montmers. All Perloo was able to gather—from the jittery chatter of his Felbart warrior guards—was that the Montmer army had been sighted, and had pitched a camp close by. It was, he knew, merely a matter of time before a challenge was issued, presumably next early.

The weather continued to moderate, turning the soft powdery, blizzard snow into stuff of a heavier, more packable weight. The Felbarts used this to their advantage, working constantly to strengthen their fortifications.

That moon-glow, Perloo, along with the rest of the Felbart army, remained outside. Tucked deep within his warm smock he slept sporadically. He did not even bother to stick out a warning ear. What was there to be warned about—he thought—other than his ultimate doom?

Perloo dreamed of his snug burrow. How he longed to be there again! At other times he started awake with a beating heart, and gave way to doleful musings about his life. In so doing he resigned himself to the notion that he would have to fight, that in all probability he would lose, that by next moon-glow he would be dead.

BERWIG AND SENYOUS PLOT

IT WAS LATE sun-glow when the Montmer army—Senyous still in the lead—arrived at the Felbart borders. Felbart scouts were sighted, but there had been no resistance to the army's advance. Even this did little to raise the low spirits of the Montmer troops. Ever since rumors had spread that the army was going to attack the Felbart stronghold, warriors were on edge. Though Berwig and Senyous had promised an easy victory, many were already saying the war was a mistake.

Senyous called a scout to his side. "How far are we from the Felbart den?"

"Not far."

"Set up the camp."

The Montmer army came to a halt. The troops arrayed themselves in a circle. In the middle of the circle a tent was erected for Berwig and Senyous. The rest of the army slipped into their smocks, burrowed into the snow and drew their smock strings tightly, then gave themselves over to unsettled sleep.

Inside the central tent a fire was made for warmth

and light. Berwig lay back upon a mound of furs eating compulsively from pots of grains, honey, and preab. At the far side Senyous—who refused to eat—appeared to be studying maps of the area. In fact he alternated stealing glances at Berwig with glances at the dragonfly wing pike. Senyous was pleased that it was so sharp.

"Oh, Great Granter," he said when Berwig finished eating, had yawned and lowered his bulk upon his pillows. "Have you worked out a war plan?"

Berwig gave himself a scratch. "Oh," he suggested casually, "we'll just attack."

Senyous gritted his teeth. "Yes, but how?"

Berwig plucked up a piece of scented preab, and rammed it into his mouth. Perfectly aware he was annoying Senyous and enjoying it, Berwig squinted at the tent ceiling.

"I don't know," he answered lazily. "Just chase them away, I suppose."

"You'll have to come up with something better than that."

Berwig yawned again. "I thought the point of all this was to get support from my tribe, not really to fight."

"Granter, they won't support you unless you win."

Berwig shrugged. "This war was your idea, Senyous, not mine. You never mentioned *winning*."

"You must win, Granter," Senyous hissed.

Berwig closed his eyes. "I'll think of something," he murmured.

"Granter," Senyous said between clenched teeth, "tomorrow we attack."

"Senyous, if you're in such a rush, you think of something," Berwig said. "What's the point of your being first assistant if you don't assist?"

"I have thought of something," Senyous returned after a moment.

"What a surprise," Berwig drawled, scratching himself between his ears.

"What," Senyous asked softly, "if they offer a challenge?"

There, thought Berwig. That's what he wants. "Do you think they might?" he asked.

"It's customary," Senyous said.

"Fine," said Berwig. "I like conventional things. If they make the offer, get someone to answer it."

"It is the attacking army that normally issues a challenge," Senyous said. "To protect Montmer honor, to protect your honor, we must challenge them."

Berwig was now quite certain what Senyous was getting at. "That doesn't trouble me," he murmured. "Any Felbart who is stupid enough to stand up to any one of us will be sent hopping fast enough."

"My, my, Granter. You are brave," Senyous hissed.

"Just write up the challenge," Berwig said in a sleepy voice. "Let someone good answer it."

"To be sure," Senyous said softly. "Which means— of course—your name will be on it. That's standard."

Berwig smiled to himself. "Of course, *me*," he said, pretending to drift off to sleep.

Senyous watched Berwig carefully . . . was he really asleep? Senyous wondered, or just pretending? Did he mean what he had said? He rather thought he did. Stupid stumphead, Senyous thought.

Quietly he hopped to his small traveling desk, took out a leaf of bark, dipped his writing stick into the flame and wrote:

To: The Felbart Packmaster
From: Berwig the Big

I, Berwig, Montmer Granter, having come this far into Felbart territory without any resistance, pronounce all of you to be cowards. Furthermore, I, Berwig, Montmer Granter, do herewith challenge your best warrior to fight against me!

Writing done, Senyous looked to see if Berwig was still sleeping. He seemed to be.

Senyous limped to the tent entrance. "Ho, warrior!" he called softly.

A warrior stuck his head into the tent and pulled an ear.

"How is the army doing?" Senyous asked.

"With great respect, Senyous," the warrior said, "they think this war is a mistake."

"Never mind what they think," Senyous said. "Everything is under control. Trust me. Just take this challenge," said Senyous. "Guard it with your life.

Tomorrow early, when we meet the Montmers, you are to go before the entire army and read it. Take another with you to carry the pine branch, the signal for a safe parley."

"I understand," the warrior said. He took the challenge, pulled an ear, and retreated.

Senyous watched him go, then hopped to his bed. Tomorrow I shall be granter, he thought and drifted off to sleep.

The moment Berwig was certain Senyous was asleep, he eased himself out of bed. Hopping quietly, he went to the tent entrance and poked his head out.

"Warrior!" he whispered.

The same warrior who had answered Senyous's summons appeared.

"How is the army doing?" Berwig asked.

"With great respect, Granter," the warrior said, "They think this war is a mistake."

"Give me what Senyous gave you."

The warrior offered up the bark sheet.

"What did he tell you to do with it?"

The warrior told him.

"Fine. Excellent. Now wait."

Berwig went back into the tent. After taking up another sheet of bark, and charring his writing stick he rewrote Senyous's challenge.

"There," Berwig said, handing the new challenge to the waiting warrior. "Now you're to do exactly what Senyous told you to do. Trust me. All will go well."

The warrior pulled his ear and left.

Berwig, very pleased with himself, went back to bed. I'll be rid of Senyous very soon, he thought. Then, as he fell contentedly asleep, he allowed himself the pleasure of thinking about being safely home again in the Central Tribe Burrow.

LUCABARA IN THE CELL

CHAPTER 29

AT THE BOTTOM of the Central Tribe Burrow, Lucabara made arrangements to dig out of the cell. First she posted Rembury by the door, getting her to press both her ears against it, trusting she would be able to pick up any sound of guard activity beyond.

Then she led four of the strongest prisoners—including Chef Fergink—up against the wood paneling, as far from the door as possible.

"There must be some board with a crack," Lucabara said. "We need to find it."

Though it took a while a crack was found. Lucabara placed her three companions next to it then attempted to wedge her fingers and claws in.

It was difficult, frustrating work, poking and prying, pulling at bits and pieces of the wood. Lucabara struggled until her paws became numb, then another took over, and another. A few pinched fingers, a cracked claw as well as a fair number of splinters resulted, but bit by bit the crack was enlarged.

When it was big enough, Lucabara got them to

pull at the crack itself, spreading it wide enough to squeeze a paw behind it.

"Got it!" she cried, managing to get a grip behind the board. Bracing herself, she heaved back. "I need someone else to get behind this too. Quickly, or my paw will be crushed!"

Fergink jammed his large paw into the crack to ease the pressure.

"Now, pull," a breathless Lucabara called.

All three hauled back. The board began to bow.

"It's going to crack," someone cried.

"Is there a guard out there?" Lucabara called to Rembury.

"Hold on!" Rembury replied. She pressed her ears against the door. "He's taking his turn . . . he's drawing closer . . . now he's hopping away . . . he's away from the door. Go!"

"Yank!" Lucabara cried.

With eight paws gripping the board, it bent farther and farther until, with a sudden *snap*, the board split in two.

All heads turned toward the door.

"I don't think the guard heard," Rembury said. "He's still hopping up and down."

Lucabara examined the hole in the paneling that had been made. "See," she whispered with excitement, "nothing but dirt behind!" She gave the earth a scratch. It crumbled with ease. "This shouldn't be hard to dig."

The prisoners worked to enlarge the hole, trying to make it big enough to allow real burrowing.

"That should do," Lucabara finally announced. Enough wood was gone so that one of them could squeeze in.

"Who's a fast burrower?" she asked.

Chef Fergink, flexing his powerful arms, hopped forward. "Let me give it a try," he said. He pulled his arms from his smock, and used the sleeves to tie it round his potbelly. Setting himself before the hole, he squared off his feet, leaned forward and began to burrow furiously. As the dirt poured from the hole the other prisoners piled it in a corner of the cell.

Fergink dug so quickly his whole head and upper body was soon leaning into the hole. Still, the earth continued to pour out. In short order Fergink's long feet stuck out from the hole. Within moments he disappeared.

It wasn't long before he poked his head out, his face, whiskers, and ears begrimed with dirt.

"I've made room for another to burrow," he announced and dove back into the hole. One of the other prisoners followed him in.

The dirt began to gush from the hole at twice the rate it had before. Those in the cell were hard-pressed to haul it away.

Fergink popped out. "Room for another," he called.

A third scrambled into the hole.

The next time Fergink reappeared, he was grinning broadly. "Lucabara," he called in an excited but low voice, "we've hit wood."

She bounded up to him. "It must be the next cell," she said. "Let me in."

Fergink backed up, and Lucabara drew herself into the hole. A rough tunnel had been made. Even so there was plenty of room for Lucabara to crawl forward until she reached the wooden wall of the adjacent cell.

"Did you hear anything from inside there?" she asked.

"Just some talking," Fergink said. "Doesn't amount to much."

Lucabara put an ear to the wall and heard the quiet murmuring. Lifting a paw she rapped smartly on the wood. The voices stopped instantly.

Lucabara pressed her mouth close to the wood. "Can you hear me in there?" she called.

At first there was only silence. Then, from the other side came a small, cautious, "Who is that?"

"Rescue," Lucabara replied. "We're Berwig's prisoners too. We've burrowed over from the cell next to yours. We need to join up.

"Listen closely," she continued. "We're going to push against the wood. You'll see it bulge. Help us by pulling in on it. We need to break through."

"Fine," came the response. "We're ready."

Lucabara looked to Fergink and the other burrowers. "Lend a paw," she said.

The three others positioned themselves next to Lucabara. Together, they began to push against the paneling. Gradually a whole section of the wood began to bend and buckle until it broke into the room with such suddenness that Lucabara tumbled onto the floor of the cell.

She looked up. A room full of prisoners was gazing down at her.

After dusting herself off, and helping Fergink hop into the cell, Lucabara informed the prisoners about what was happening in the world outside. She also told them her plan to gather all prisoners together, arm themselves, lead an uprising in the Central Tribe Burrow, then depose Gumpel before the army returned from the war.

"It's risky," a prisoner pointed out. "But I'm for it. Stay here and we'll just rot." The other prisoners agreed.

By the time Lucabara got back to the central cell, work was already progressing on breaking through to the cell on the other side. The process was the same as before, and just as successful. It was not long before almost fifty prisoners had joined together.

The question then became, what next to do.

"I think," suggested Fergink, "we should just beat the door down and make a hop for it."

"I'm not so sure that's wise," Rembury said. "The noise will bring other warriors. Better wait until someone comes in. Then we can overpower them with ease."

This plan was agreed upon. While the prisoners set about to wait impatiently another of them kept his ears against the door, listening. "Shhh!" he finally cried.

All heads turned toward him.

"I think they're bringing food."

"To either side of the door," Lucabara urged. "They mustn't see us when they come in. Hop it!"

There was a mad scramble as the prisoners leaped into position. All became quiet, save for nervous breathing, and the twitching of ears.

The door opened. Two warriors—one carrying a bowl of moldy preab, the other a pike—peered in. Seeing no one, they became puzzled and took another hop into the room. No sooner did they than there was a great shout from the prisoners. Taken by surprise the armed warrior had his pike ripped away by Fergink.

Lucabara was at the open door. "Follow me," she cried, and began bounding down the hallways. Pouring from the cell, the freed prisoners began hopping madly after her.

THE ARMIES MEET

IT WAS EARLY when Perloo woke from his final doze. Releasing his smock string he opened his baggy eyes and was treated to a wondrous sun-up. Streaks of orange, pink, and blue filled the sky. The colors reflected upon the snow, causing it to sparkle as if a rainbow had shattered and the bits lay scattered on the earth. The trees seemed afire. Then he saw the sun itself rise, a great, poppy-red ball of flame. It made him think of one of his favorite Mogwat sayings: "Nothing in the world is so small that the sun cannot warm it."

"Oh, sun," Perloo prayed, "warm my heart."

Suddenly, there was a shout from some Felbart warriors. "They've arrived!" came the cry.

Sure enough, the Montmer army, strung out in a line that ran parallel to the Felbart ramparts, was hopping in perfect unison over a ridge, then down upon the open plain before the Felbart walls.

The large force was splendid in polished wood armor and foot guards. As the Montmers hopped their slow, deliberate hops, they clacked their pikes against their armor, creating an ominious "crack-crack-crack!" that rattled the air.

From their ramparts the Felbarts watched in silence and not a little awe. Perloo himself was enthralled, hardly knowing what to feel, pride or fear. "Oh, my, my," he whispered to himself. Here was a mighty force of Montmers indeed! How strange, he thought, to be a part of history, even as he was about to be overwhelmed by it.

Only when he shifted slightly did Perloo realize that Packmaster Weyanto had come to stand by his side.

"A powerful force," Weyanto growled tensely.

The Montmers continued to hop forward until they drew within a hundred hops of the Felbart walls. There they stopped and stood in a line parallel to the wall, near enough so that Perloo and the Felbarts could look down and see their faces with perfect clarity.

Hopping near the head of the army was Berwig— all puffed up. In the actual lead was Senyous, looking small. Both were in armor. Berwig's armor was resplendent, inlaid wood with bits of gold and sparkling mica. The effect was spoiled only when he scratched himself.

His squinty eyes were intense, his gaze shifting here, there, taking in the Felbart walls as well as the warriors atop them. He was also stealing glances at Senyous.

Senyous's armor was quite drab, having no refinements or decorations. But to Perloo's surprise it was

Senyous—not Berwig—who held the Montmer dragonfly wing pike of leadership. The old Montmer kept his features averted, clearly more interested in Berwig than the enemy troops before him.

Neither one, Perloo suspected, realized he was on the Felbart ramparts looking down at them.

Before the Montmer leaders were two Montmer warriors. One held a branch of pine in her paws.

Having come close to the Felbart walls, the Montmer army began to hop up and down in place and beat their armor.

The Felbarts, atop the ramparts, responded by striking the butt ends of their bone clubs against their bibs and lifting their snouts to bark and yelp. Some beat drums. The air was full of clatter and confusion.

Abruptly, Senyous held up his dragonfly pike. The Montmer army became still. It also served to quiet the Felbarts. The two silent armies gazed at each other across the snowy plain.

Perloo sensed that the Montmers were somewhat taken aback by the numbers of Felbart warriors as well as the height of the snow walls. At the same time he detected that the Felbarts were unnerved by the size of the Montmer army as well as its fierce appearance.

The Montmer warrior with the pine branch took twelve hops forward. "We come in the name of peace!" she called.

"Share your name!" was the barked reply from one of the Felbart commanders.

The second Montmer warrior hopped forward.

"My name is Wexagut of the mighty Montmer tribe," he cried.

"Wexagut," the Felbart commander replied, "my name is Qualamor, of the ever victorious Felbarts. What brings you to our den?"

"I bring a message from our great granter to your self-styled packmaster."

"Our packmaster is willing to hear what your presumptuous granter wishes to say."

"Berwig the Big seeks to avoid spilling Felbart blood. Therefore, he generously offers a challenge."

"Packmaster Weyanto," came the equally formal return, "mighty warrior that he is, fears no challenge. Still, he wishes to prevent Montmer misery. Read your challenge so all may hear it."

Wexagut came forward three extra hops and drew out a sheet of bark. Holding the sheet with two paws he began to read slowly and clearly.

To: The Felbart Packmaster

I, Senyous, First Assistant to the Granter, having come this far into Felbart Territory without any resistance, pronounce all of you to be cowards. Further more, I, Senyous, First Assistant to the Granter, do herewith challenge your best warrior to fight against me!

So say I, Senyous, First Assistant

When the Montmer warrior read the first, "I, Senyous," Senyous let out a bleating screech that was heard across the field. His face a knot of rage, he whirled about and glared at Berwig.

A smug Berwig looked back at the little fellow and snorted.

Once the challenge had been read, the Montmers resumed hopping up and down and beating their armor, as if to taunt the Felbarts. The Felbarts, in turn, lifted their snouts and resumed yelping, barking, and howling.

Senyous quickly recovered from his shock. Brandishing the dragonfly pike, he hopped forward in his limping, bent-back way. Standing before the Felbart ramparts he began to twirl and manipulate his pike as if it were some feather wand, and his paws had twice the normal fingers.

Perloo felt a tap on his shoulder. It was Weyanto. "There is your challenge," he said solemnly. "Do as you said you would. Defeat the Montmer and you will have done much to end this war." So saying he gave Perloo a nudge forward.

"But. . . . but," Perloo stammered, "it's Senyous!"

"Whoever it is," Weyanto said, "you must meet him."

Perloo could hardly breathe, much less move.

"Perloo, keep your promise," the packmaster growled.

Virtually every Felbart warrior on the ramparts was staring angrily at Perloo. He knew then he had but little choice: Stay and be clubbed to death by the Felbarts, or be poked to death by Senyous's pike.

Even as he stood there not knowing what to do, two Felbart warriors grabbed him by his arms, and dragged him to the top of the icy chute that led from the top of the ramparts to the field below where Senyous was waiting.

Like an old bundle the hapless Perloo was placed at the top of the chute, made to sit, and then given a shove. Holding on to his pike with trembling paws, long feet sticking straight up, Perloo slid down onto the field.

IN THE CENTRAL TRIBE BURROW

IN THE CENTRAL Tribe Burrow the Great Hall was deserted. Though it was time for early meal, the eating tables were empty. A few bowls were scattered here and there but they contained only partially eaten food from the previous meals. The fireplaces were cold. Staleness, dank and heavy, hovered in the air. By order of Gumpel.

Only a few candles were lit, their light yellow and feeble, so they seemed to cast more shadow than light. By order of Gumpel.

The doors to the Great Hall were latched shut. The sole way to get in was by the main doors and there, two warriors hopped back and forth preventing entry. By order of Gumpel.

"What time did she say she would be here?" one of the warriors asked the other. She kept her voice low, knowing that loud speaking was not acceptable to the new granter. The second one shrugged. "Soon."

"Different, isn't she?" the first said cautiously.

"Not what you'd call social," said the other.

"Doesn't want much going on."

They hopped back and forth.

"Any word about the war?" one asked the other.

"Nothing."

"I wonder what will happen now? Jolaine's death—"

The warrior, making a nervous glance about, said, "Murder."

"Well, then, murder. Then Berwig as granter. Freedoms suspended. The war. This Gumpel creature taking over."

"It's anybody's guess," said the other. He paused in his hopping. "Shhh!" he cautioned. "I think she's coming."

The two warriors listened intently. There was a faint, flop, flop, flop. Someone was hopping sluggishly in their direction.

"It's her," one of the warriors said.

Like a worm creeping out from beneath sodden leaves, Gumpel emerged from the shadows. Now and again she paused, gazed about, rubbed her eyes, adjusted her smock, sniffed the air, yawned, making it clear that time was of no importance to her.

The warriors pulled their ears.

Gumpel looked around and nodded. "The doors," she whispered.

The warriors sprang to unlatch them.

"Slowly, slowly!" she cautioned.

Just as she was about to enter the hall, she paused. "Is anybody about?" she asked.

"No one, Granter. According to your orders everybody is in their burrow rooms."

"Are the doors to the Great Hall latched?"

"No one can get in without our letting them."

"Good," Gumpel muttered. "It's better that way. Everyone in their proper rooms. No bustle. No noise. Easier to keep track of them all. Now, no one is to come in here. No one. I have things to do."

The warriors pulled their ears.

Gumpel hopped lethargically into the hall. The doors behind her closed softly. Once inside she stood still, listening to the silence, breathing deeply, nodding and smiling to herself, occasionally wiping her nose with the back of her paw.

"All mine!" she muttered to herself. "Every little bit." She allowed herself a sigh of satisfaction. "I do what I want. When I want. Smile at this one. Frown at that. Punish whom I will. Whatever I order *happens.*" She gave herself a hug with her stubby arms.

Near the Settop she stopped and looked about. Jolaine's proclamation—as rewritten by Senyous—was still posted on the wall.

With care she removed the bark sheet from the wall and carried it to the Settop. Once there she sat down, and placed the proclamation on the floor before her. She gazed at it, silently.

Gumpel studied the proclamation, reading and rereading it. From time to time she turned the sheet of bark one way or another. At one point she got off the Settop and pressed her face close to the sheet. She saw the line that joined the two parts of the proclamation. "That Senyous," Gumpel murmured to herself. "What a wily fellow."

Vacantly, she gazed about, wondering what was happening in the war. "Something will happen. One won't be back. Maybe," she said with a small smile, "maybe, all of them will die."

She turned back to the proclamation. Placing one paw on one side of the crack and the other paw on the other side, she pressed down hard and carefully pulled the sheets apart.

Now there were two pieces of proclamation before her. Which, she wondered, was Jolaine's original? By way of an answer, she asked herself another question: Which half was better for Berwig and Senyous? The left half. Gumpel shredded it then flung the bits away.

"If Senyous could rewrite this, so can I," she said. "But this time it should be in my favor. What it should say is that Jolaine proclaimed me granter."

In her mind she began to compose a sentence.

Since I, Jolaine, have the right,
to proclaim anyone in the clan as
Granter I say Gumpel should be the one!

JOLAINE

Gumpel liked the sentence so much she repeated it fifteen times. Each time she did so she found it more to her liking.

She looked about. All she needed was some bark and a writing stick. "Guard," she called.

There was no answer.

"Guard!" she called again.

Grumbling with annoyance, trying to think of some harsh punishment for such disobedience, Gumpel hopped lethargically toward the door.

She was halfway there when the doors burst open. A crowd of more than fifty Montmers stood on the threshold. All were armed with pikes. Before them stood Lucabara.

Gumpel peered at them. "Who . . . who are you?" she demanded.

"My name is Lucabara. We've come to free the Settop."

Gumpel looked around. "Free the Settop?" she said in soft bewilderment. "But I am Gumpel. *I'm* the granter. Jolaine said so. I'll have to punish you all."

It was Lucabara who cried, "She's with Berwig and Senyous. Seize her!"

The crowd, brandishing their pikes, pressed into the hall. Gumpel began to hop back. "Oh, no, not at all," she said. "I'm the granter. I'm the one who—" Abruptly, she turned, and began to hop frantically away from the crowd toward the doors at the far end of the hall.

"Catch her!" Lucabara cried.

The Montmers hopped off in pursuit.

Gumpel reached the far doors first only to find— by her orders—them latched. With a shriek she whirled about, and tried for another set of doors. They too were locked. "Save me!" she cried and hopped in yet another direction.

The Montmers followed. Every time they closed in on her she eluded them by bounding from one side of the hall to another, until she was finally trapped cowering beneath a table. "I'm the granter! I am! Nobody but me!" she continued to protest as she was dragged before Lucabara and the rest of the escaped prisoners.

"Who gave you the right to sit on the Settop?" Lucabara demanded.

Gumpel shrank down. She began to blubber.

"Answer!"

"Berwig did. But only until he came back."

"What's that you have in your paw?" Lucabara suddenly asked.

"Oh, this," mumbled Gumpel. "Just a sheet of nothing."

Lucabara held out her paw. "Give it to us," she demanded.

Gumpel sighed. "If you insist."

Lucabara took the sheet and gave it a quick scrutiny. "It's the other half of Jolaine's final proclamation!" she exclaimed. The excited crowd pressed around to see for themselves.

"And the other half?" Fergink asked.

"Here it is," Lucabara said pulling it from her smock.

She lay the two pieces side by side atop the Settop.
All the Montmers crowded around and read it.

*Whereas I, Granter Jolaine, sixty-third Granter
in the noble line of Tornagerty the First, have
come to the end of my life,*

*And whereas, I, Granter Jolaine, wish the Montmer
Mountain tribe to go forward in the pursuit of
freedom:*

*And whereas, my only cub Berwig, appears bent
on restoring old, absolutist ways, and seeks to
take back the old Granter power unto himself:*

*And whereas, I, Granter Jolaine, have the right,
by ancient law to proclaim anyone in the Tribe
as Granter,*

*I, Granter Jolaine, hereby proclaim Perloo to be
my successor with all the rights and privileges of
Granter, with the hope and expectation that he
will preserve and enlarge the freedom of every
Montmer.*

JOLAINE

"You see," Lucabara cried, "Perloo really is
granter."

Suddenly someone shouted out, "But where's Gumpel?"

She was gone—fled from the hall and burrow—not to be seen again.

"It doesn't matter," Lucabara assured them. "Perloo is granter."

"But why isn't he here, now?" asked someone. "What's he doing?"

THE CHALLENGE

NEAR THE SUMMIT of Rasquich Mountain Perloo's heart was pounding. The palms of his trembling paws were wet with fear. The hair upon his body prickled. Behind him on the high ramparts were the Felbart warriors—as well as Packmaster Weyanto—all of whom were watching him intently. Before him was ranged the Montmer army with Berwig before it.

Right before Perloo stood Senyous. Small and wiry, his face contorted with venom, the old Montmer began to hop forward.

As Perloo, moving with tiny hops, went toward his foe, the only noise he heard was the flat of their feet against the snow and his own agitated breathing. When he and Senyous were just a few hops apart Perloo halted.

Suddenly, Senyous began to flaunt his pike—twirling it in an elaborate, impressive figure—while shrieking, "It is I, Senyous the Sly, of the Montmer tribe who offer this challenge. Who among my enemies accepts it?"

Summoning all his strength, Perloo replied, "I suppose it must be me. Because I'm Perloo, the true granter."

His words caused a sensation among the Montmer army. Whispering rippled through the ranks. Ears twitched and trembled. Noses quivered. Even Berwig squinted at Perloo as if not believing what he was seeing or hearing. His ears shook violently. He began to scratch himself with fury, wishing that, after all, he had given the challenge. How much better for him to defeat his enemy on his own.

Senyous was momentarily taken aback. He leaned forward the better to see Perloo, his mouth agape with astonishment. His ears shook. He allowed his pike to touch the ground.

The next moment, however, he jerked himself up so that, for Senyous, he stood tall. Then he offered a malicious grin. Here was great luck indeed! Nothing could be better. He would deal with Perloo himself. It would establish his opportunity to vanquish Perloo. Then he would kill Berwig.

"Perloo," he cried out in his thin, reedy voice, "I welcome your acceptance of my challenge! What pleasure to prove that you're false. What delight I'll take in defeating you. I call you by your rightful name, Perloo the Betrayer!"

With that he put his pike through yet another series of rapid, complex figures, then hopped forward, eager to begin the deadly combat.

Perloo, despite his best intention, retreated a few

hops back. Then he looked out across the snowy plain toward the Montmer army. "I . . . I *am* Perloo!" he shouted at them. "Just before Jolaine died of old age —not murder—she called me to her side. She said she didn't trust Berwig to become granter. She said she was fearful he would take away our freedoms. That he might make war upon the Felbarts."

"Liar!" cried Berwig.

Perloo went on. "Tribal law says the dying granter may choose the new granter. She chose me. I'm your true granter."

"Nonsense!" Berwig bellowed. "*I* am the granter. No one else but me. Don't listen to Perloo. He's nothing. A nobody. Senyous, hurry up and kill him!"

All during Perloo's brief speech Senyous never shifted his wrath-filled eyes away from Perloo. Now he took another limping hop forward. "No more talk, traitor!" he shouted. "Answer the Montmer challenge with your pike!" So saying he took another hop forward, closing the gap between Perloo and him even more. "For it is I who should be the true granter!"

Berwig, hearing this, started. His nose turned crimson. His ears began to shake. He desired nothing less than for Perloo and Senyous to kill each other.

Perloo, wanting desperately only to hold his place and not retreat anymore, fumbled with his pike, unsure what to do. Not that Senyous gave him an opportunity to reflect. He aimed his pike right at Perloo. It was so sharp Perloo could barely see its point.

Awkwardly, Perloo stuck his pike out toward

Senyous. With something almost delicate to his movements, the old Montmer tapped it away. Perloo whacked back.

Suddenly, Senyous struck Perloo's pike to one side, made a feint to his left, jabbed toward his right. In so doing he completely baffled Perloo. But he was not done yet. With a quick stab, he poked at Perloo's armor. The wooden bib split apart like an old door and fell to the ground. Perloo, knowing at that moment Senyous could have punctured his heart, almost fainted.

But Senyous did not choose to kill him. His vanity held him back. He wanted to show off, to tease Perloo, and humiliate him before all who watched. Instead of killing him he made another complex series of maneuvers.

Grinning hideously, Senyous took another limping hop toward Perloo. "I'm going to skewer you to your Felbart walls," he snarled.

Perloo, sniffling, hacked back with his own pike. More by luck than skill he struck Senyous' pike a number of times, the success of panic. And indeed his movements were so unpredictable, so random, Senyous could not anticipate any of them. That kept Senyous at bay for a while. Within moments, however, he recovered and began to pressure Perloo backward hop by hop. He thrust at Perloo now here, now there, as if wishing to make the air around him full of holes. Having done so the old Montmer stood back and grinned, enjoying Perloo's breathless ineptitude.

Then, with a loud snort, Senyous showed off his skill again with yet another elaborate drill, twirling and shifting his pike from paw to paw as if he were only there to provide entertainment to an audience. How sweet now were all those hours of secret practice!

Hot and despairing, Perloo hacked and banged back, prodding when he could, occasionally managing a blow upon Senyous's armor that produced nothing more than a great thwacking sound. While it stirred those who were watching, it was meaningless. Senyous was not merely winning with ease, it was perfectly clear to those who watched that he could do away with Perloo at any moment he chose to do so.

Increasingly desperate, Perloo redoubled his efforts to defend himself but only grew wilder, which made Senyous cooler, deadlier.

Then, with a quick, astonishing motion—not used before—Senyous struck Perloo's pike right out of his paws.

There were gasps from both the Felbarts and the Montmer armies.

Once again Senyous could have skewered Perloo. Instead, he offered up a wicked smile, made a low, exaggerated bow, and hopped back, allowing Perloo to pick up his pike again, as if he desired to give him every chance possible.

Though close to exhaustion, there was nothing Perloo could do but take up the pike again and resume his crude defense.

Senyous pressed harder than before, forcing Perloo back and back again until his heels struck against the Felbart walls. The next moment Senyous made still another brilliant stroke, striking Perloo's pike away a second time. This time, however, he did not allow Perloo to recover it. Instead, Senyous made a lightning fast maneuver and flipped Perloo's pike even farther away. Perloo was completely without defense.

Without mercy, Senyous resumed his attack with a series of thrusts that pushed Perloo even farther up against the Felbart snow ramparts. Arms spread wide, paws clutching frantically at the snow behind him, Perloo was all but pinioned to the walls.

"What good is it being granter, Perloo," Senyous taunted, "if you can't *keep* it?"

That said, he took a backward hop, braced himself, gripped his pike with two paws—Perloo saw it all—and prepared to drive his pike deep into Perloo's chest.

In that same moment, Perloo's paws, reaching back, scooped up some snow. As fast as he ever did anything in his life, he brought his paws together, squeezed the snow into a ball, and in a continuation of the same movement, hurled the snowball right into Senyous's face. The snowball struck the first assistant right between the eyes.

Taken completely by surprise, Senyous staggered back. No one was more astonished than Perloo. For a moment he did no more than gawk. He even began to offer an apology when he realized what he had done. Seeing his chance, he scooped up more snow, and hurled more snowballs at Senyous. Each one battered Senyous's head until the old Montmer dropped his pike and sat back on the snow, stunned. Perloo hurled one more snowball that smacked the first assistant right on the nose. Hands over his face, Senyous tumbled backward and lay prostrate.

Perloo stood there, eyes blinking in astonishment. It was a voice, crying "Finish him, Perloo!" that brought him back to his senses.

Perloo hopped forward, snatched up the dragonfly wing pike, and flung it toward the Felbart walls. Gathering one more ball of snow he held it over Senyous.

"Do you give up?" he cried excitedly, cocking his arm, ready to hurl the snowball down.

Disarmed, Senyous tried to scramble away, only to receive another snowball right on the back of his head that laid him out flat. Shrieking, "I surrender! I surrender!" he burst into tears.

Perloo, utterly exhausted, rocked back on his heels and looked about. That was when he saw Berwig staring at him with amazement, his big body shaking with terror. He had fallen to his knees and had lifted his paws in supplication. "Don't hurt me!" he cried. "Please."

Perloo was so dumbfounded by Berwig's submission, that he continued to stand still, struggling to find his breath, hardly knowing what to say or do.

Berwig took the hesitation as a threat. He began to yank off his bracelets one after the other, and throw them at Perloo. "Take my things," he shouted. "They'll make you rich. Take anything you want. Just don't hurt me!"

As Perloo continued to watch in amazement, Berwig flung off his armor and tossed that too at his feet. "I renounce the grantership," he shouted. With that he flung himself down full length, face down upon the snow, and began to scratch himself furiously.

At this abdication there was a great shout of joy from both armies. The Montmers threw down their pikes and began to hop up and down. As for the Felbarts they dropped their clubs, lifted their snouts and began to bark, yelp, and howl wildly.

Perloo continued to just stand where he was, stunned by what had happened. Nor did he move until he felt a tap on his shoulder. It was Weyanto.

"Well done, Perloo," said the packmaster with a grin. "You have won. And in your own way."

AFTER THE CHALLENGE

CHAPTER 33

WEYANTO HAD BERWIG and Senyous taken
up by Felbart warriors and escorted into the den.
Perloo was not at all sure what to do. He was so tired
he could hardly stand.

"Perloo," Weyanto urged, "you really must speak to
your troops."

"Do I have to?"

"Perloo, you're truly granter now."

"I suppose . . ." Perloo murmured. He looked toward the Montmer army and fussed with his drooping whiskers. Rubbing his paws nervously, he hopped
forward.

The Montmer troops stared at him with a mix of
amazement and curiosity.

"My . . . friends," Perloo began. "As you have seen,
both Berwig and Senyous have been defeated and
captured. You need not worry. The Felbarts will treat
them well."

"And as I told you, I never murdered Jolaine.
Indeed, it was she who asked me to become

next granter. That means, I suppose, I'm your new granter now.

"The first thing I wish to do is proclaim this war to be over."

This announcement was met by cheers.

"The second thing," Perloo went on, "is to restore all freedoms to the tribe."

Another cheer.

"Finally, I think you should go back to your homes as fast as you can. Let everybody know there what has happened here.

"Now, ski quickly. It's downhill all the way. Your families and friends are waiting for you."

This too was met with a cheer.

As soon as Perloo saw the Montmer army disperse he returned to the Felbart den. The Felbarts who greeted him now did so with great respect, though he thought he detected some amusement from them as well. He chose to ignore it. What did it matter now?

He went first to Packmaster Weyanto. "Thank you for trusting me," Perloo said to him.

"Perloo," Weyanto returned, "you have kept your word. We Felbarts wish to live in peace with you Montmers. May that be the last of the Felbart–Montmer wars. With you as granter I think it may be possible. We will work together on that."

Perloo said he hoped they would.

"Now," Weyanto asked, "what do you want done with Berwig and Senyous?"

"I suppose I need to deal with them."

Berwig and Senyous had been placed in the same crowded cell in which Perloo was imprisoned. Perloo went in alone, shutting the door behind him.

Senyous was squatting on the ground hunched up, paws clasped around his knees. Berwig, also squatting, was as far away from his partner as the room allowed, alternatingly stuffing his mouth with preab and scratching himself.

At first neither paid any attention to Perloo. Only after he stood for a while in silence did Senyous turn toward him and sneer, "I should have killed you when I had the chance."

"Oh, well," Perloo offered. "I'm glad you didn't."

"I'm the one who should have been granter!" Senyous shouted. "It takes cunning as well as intelligence to be granter. Neither of you have any while I have both."

That roused Berwig. "You're a nothing," he shouted. "Defeated by a pup throwing a *snowball!*" he snorted.

"At least I fought," Senyous countered. "You just gave up!"

"Cheat! Liar!" Berwig threw back.

Then Perloo said, "And what shall be done with you?" he asked Senyous.

"Do what you want," Senyous sulked.

"And you?" Perloo said to Berwig.

The big fellow looked around and scratched himself. "I'm the cub of a granter. I should be treated with respect."

"I suppose I could leave you with the Felbarts," Perloo offered. "Let them decide."

"No!" Senyous shouted.

"Not that!" Berwig begged.

"Or," Perloo offered, "if you promise to have nothing more to do with each other or try to claim power and live in peace, you can return home."

"Don't worry about that," Senyous snarled. "I don't wish to ever see Berwig again. What good is that stump brain to me? As for returning home, I'd rather wander than live under your grantership."

"Do as you wish," Perloo said. "And you?" he asked Berwig.

"Oh, I'll find some abandoned burrow," Berwig whined. "I'll live simply and quietly. Keep bees. Collect honey."

Senyous snorted.

"As far as I'm concerned," Perloo said, "you can do what you want."

When both Berwig and Senyous mumbled their agreement Perloo returned to Weyanto.

"And now?" asked the Packmaster.

"I'd best go home."

"To be granter, Perloo?"

"I will have to decide."

PERLOO THE BOLD

WHEN PERLOO TOOK his leave of Felbart territory the day was brilliant, clear, and crisp. The snow
underfoot was fast. As he skied down the mountain
the wind in his face made him feel as if he were
glowing. His legs and thighs, moving with the terrain,
gave him a feeling of gracefulness, a thing Perloo did
not experience very often.

What should I do? he kept asking himself. Should
I be granter? Or should I not? He recalled Mogwat's
saying, "A life without challenge is a life not lived."
Just as quickly he recalled another: "Of all challenges
the greatest is to be yourself."

Perloo brought himself to a sharp stop and looked
out through the trees toward the mountains. The
whole world seemed to be glowing with life.

"What do *I* want to do?" he wondered out loud.

He thought of his burrow rooms. He thought of
his books. He thought of the Great Hall in the
Central Tribe Burrow. And the Settop. He thought of
Jolaine. He thought too of Lucabara. "What *do* I want
to do?" he asked himself again.

Then he recalled what Jolaine had named him, "Perloo the Unwilling." He even said it to himself out loud a few times. *"Perloo the Unwilling. Perloo the Unwilling. Perloo the Unwilling."* By the time he had said it the third time he knew exactly what he would do.

It was past middle when Perloo arrived at the main doors of the Central Tribal Burrow. He went through the open doors, past the entryway, and into the Great Hall itself.

The hall—crowded with many eating at the tables—was not unlike the time when he and Lucabara first came there together. Hearth fires were blazing. Candles were bright. Sounds of munching and gnawing filled the air.

Perloo chose not to announce himself. Instead he began to slowly hop through the hall. Suddenly, he halted. There on the wall he saw Jolaine's proclamation posted. It was whole and complete. Lucabara, he knew, must have done it. The tribe knew the truth.

Sure enough, as he hopped along, flop, flop, flop, the Great Hall became very quiet. One after another Montmers rose from their places, pulled their ears, and watched him go by.

Perloo nodded back as amiably as he could. As he approached the Settop, he saw Lucabara and stopped. She grinned at him.

"Lucabara—" he began to say.

"Shhh!" she interrupted. "We can talk later. But first . . ." She drew herself up, tried to look very serious, made something of a bow, and even pulled her left ear.

"Granter Perloo," she intoned, "welcome home. News of your great victory has already been shared. Better yet, news of your first orders have come. History shall know you as Perloo the Bold." So saying Lucabara pulled her ears again in a show of respect, but she could not keep from smiling broadly.

There was a shout of approval and much pulling of ears.

Perloo hardly knew what to say. He hopped closer to Lucabara. "I don't think I can . . ."

Lucabara reached out and turned him around. "Go to the Settop," she whispered. "Speak to the tribe."

Perloo, his nose turning red, hopped toward the Settop. He glanced at the image of Mogwat, then turned and held up a paw. A hush came upon the hall.

For a moment he stood nervously worrying his paws, and fussing with his scruffy whiskers. "My friends," he began, "you have honored me with your ears. I gather you know—thanks to Lucabara—that Jolaine proclaimed me granter. She never asked me for my opinion. It was a complete surprise."

That said, Perloo took a deep breath, fussed with his whiskers, and said, "But I have decided not to become granter."

There were cries of "No, no. You must be!"

Perloo rubbed his paws nervously. "No, I'm just not suited to it. As you may now know it's the right of all granters—by law and tradition—to abdicate, to choose their successor. As for who should succeed me, I don't have much doubt. It should be *all* of you.

"Let there be no more granters. Whatever happens to the Montmer tribe will have to be decided by everyone."

The hall erupted with joy. Never had there been so much cheering. Even Lucabara, as surprised as any, hopped over to Perloo. "Oh, Perloo," she said, "you really are what you are." And she gave him a great hug. His nose turned the deepest shade of red ever.

It was not until moon-glow that Perloo was able to make his way back to his own burrow. He let himself in by the front door, then stumbled about the dark searching for his flints. After some fumbling he made a spark and lit his candle.

He looked about. The burrow was just as he had left it. Even the book—*The Way of Montmer Heroes*—lay on his moss bed exactly as he had left it.

Not even bothering to light a fire, Perloo sighed and climbed into his bed, adjusted the pillow, found his place in the book, and started to read.

Then, lo! Mighty Muldark the Murky, rose up and smote the fearful Felbart a murderous thrust as loud as thunder and as swift as lightning. Blood billowed like a tumbling brook.

"Oh, mighty Montmer!" cried the dying Felbart.

"Thou hast slain me in fair and most chilling challenge. But yea, I have besworn to struggle on forever lest I . . .

Perloo's baggy eyes began to close. "That's *not* the way it is," he murmured. "Besides, I am very . . . sleepy. . . ." The book slipped from his paws. In moments he was fast asleep—dreaming his own dreams.

THE SAYINGS OF

If you learn to know your enemy before you hate him, you may learn not to have an enemy.

Too often a Montmer will take one today over three yesterdays and two tomorrows.

To see the world with the eyes of others is to stand atop a new mountain.

Knowing the length of a Montmer's ear won't tell you if he can listen.

Better to live with ten Montmers in uneasy peace than one in a war.

When you take one backward hop it requires two hops to go forward.

You are never more alone than when you are followed by many.

Fear not the weak, only they who try to hide their weaknesses.

Nothing in the world so small that the sun cannot warm it.

MOGWAT THE MAGPIE

Truth is often painful to speak but soothing to live.

Of all things, the hardest to keep is a promise.

Lies fly then fall. Truth hops but keeps going.

Of all challenges the greatest is to be yourself.

They who pine for the past, fear the future.

A life without challenge is a life not lived.

Life is given. The rest one gives oneself.

Ignorance is the cruelest weather.

Only the dead have no choices.

The future begins in the past.

ABOUT THE AUTHOR

AVI IS THE AUTHOR of over thirty books for young people, including fiction for older readers, chapter books, a picture book, and a short story collection. Among his many awards are the Christopher Medal, two Newbery Honor Book citations, and the Boston Globe/Horn Book Award, and his books are on many state master reading lists. Formerly a librarian, Avi is now a full-time writer living in Denver, Colorado.